A Mew Beginning

A Whales and Tails Mystery

by
Kathi Daley

Whales and Tails

Romeow and Juliet
The Mad Catter
Grimm's Furry Tail
Much Ado About Felines
The Legend of Tabby Hollow
The Cat of Christmas Past
The Tail of Two Tabbies
The Great Catsby
Count Catula
The Cat of Christmas Present
A Winters Tail
Taming of the Tabby
Frankencat
The Cat of Christmas Future
Farewell to Felines
The Catsgiving Feast
A Whale of a Tail
The Catnap Before Christmas
A Mew Beginning

Chapter 1

Wednesday, April 1

We've all had them. Those moments when disquiet slowly creeps into our consciousness, expanding and mutating until it eventually redefines itself as anxiety that consumes our every thought. This apprehension often comes on gradually, beginning as a feeling of unease that builds slowly and steadily, until it grows into a sense of foreboding, demanding that we stop what we're doing and pay attention.

"Cait. Are you in there?"

I looked up at my best friend, Tara O'Brian, who was waving a hand in front of my face. "I'm here."

"Is everything okay?"

I looked around the dining room of the newest eatery in town, The Wild Rose Café, where we'd arranged to meet for lunch. For a moment, I'd almost forgotten where I was. I really did need to get a grip. "I'm fine."

"It seems like you're a million miles away."

I took a deep breath and forced my mind to refocus on the conversation we'd been having. "I guess I've been distracted lately with everything that's been going on. Between the explosion at the bookstore, the move out of my cabin and into Mr. Parsons' house, and my new job helping Cody at the newspaper, I feel somewhat displaced."

"That's understandable. I've been feeling much the same way. I'm hanging in there just fine, but I will be glad when we can reopen the store."

"You were telling me about your conversation with the insurance company. Are we making any progress?"

She shook her head slowly. "In a nutshell, we're still waiting for the money I've been assured is due to us to be released. It's been three and a half months. I can't believe how long this is taking. In the beginning, I actually assumed Coffee Cat Books would be repaired and open for business by this point."

I placed my hand over Tara's. "I know. I'm sorry. Neither of us had any idea how long the investigation would delay things, and I'm not sure either of us realized how much the whole process would disrupt our lives."

She bowed her head. "I guess there isn't anything we can do other than what we're doing. It will be fine. We'll get through this, and at some point, the insurance company is going to have to make good on our policy and settle our claim."

Tara and I had decided that the problem with our claim was that the source of the fire had been a bomb that was intentionally detonated by a seriously disturbed man who had set out on a mission to destroy Santa Claus. Because the damage to the bookstore hadn't been caused by anything as simple as a lightning strike or electrical problem, an investigation into the cause had been warranted. The insurance company had told Tara that they hoped to offset their loss by suing the man responsible for the explosion. I had my doubts that they'd get anything out of the guy, especially since he was going to spend much, if not all, of the rest of his life in prison, but they seemed determined to try, and until they had exhausted all options available to them, they seemed determined not to pay us the money we both felt we were due.

"It has been frustrating," Tara added as she stirred a teaspoon of sugar into her iced tea. "But I've enjoyed working with Danny and Aiden at the bar."

Aiden and Danny Hart were my older brothers. They'd pooled their resources a while back and bought O'Malley's Bar. They'd kept the name, but they'd fully remodeled the place and made it their own.

"Did Aiden decide to go on the fishing trip he'd been invited to join?"

Aiden and Danny had both made their living on the sea prior to selling their boats and opening the bar, but as far as I was concerned, they both still have saltwater in their veins. Aiden had been invited on a fishing expedition down south, but as far as I knew, he hadn't decided whether or not he was going to go.

"He did," Tara confirmed. "As you know, it's the offseason here on the island, so the bar is slow anyway, and with the bookstore closed, Cassie and I are both available to help out during the busy times, so Danny managed to convince him this was as good a time as any to be away."

"I'm glad he went. It seemed like he needed a break."

Tara nodded. "I feel like Aiden is happy with his choice to sell the boat and buy the bar, but it does seem he needs to get out there on the water every now and again to keep his sanity. He left for San Diego yesterday. I guess he's meeting up with his friend today, and they planned to head out to sea tomorrow. He thought he might be gone about a month."

"Good for him. I hope he has a wonderful time." In a way, it felt odd that Tara knew more about what was going on with my brothers than I did, but she worked at the bar with them, so she saw them every day, and she was in a seriously *on-again* phase in her *on-again/off-again* relationship with my brother, Danny. While she hadn't said as much, based on my own observations, I had the feeling that they were pretty much living together. I really hoped it worked out this time. In my opinion, Tara and Danny had hurt each other more than any two people ought to, but then again, I really believed they loved each other more than a lot of couples I knew.

Tara glanced at her watch. "I should get going. I told Danny I'd come in early today to help with the inventory before the bar opens."

"Yeah, I should get going as well. Cody left early this morning to go over to San Juan Island to interview a guy who claims to know something about the series of missing persons cases in the area, but he should be back by now."

"Why is Cody interviewing him? It seems like knowing something about missing persons is the sort of thing Finn and the sheriff should be looking into." My brother-in-law, Ryan Finnegan, Finn to his friends, is the resident deputy for the island we'd both lived on our entire lives.

"They've tried to talk to the guy, but either he doesn't actually know anything, or he has a problem with cops and isn't telling everything he knows. The fact that the guy might have information about the missing women came from a tip that was provided by a bartender on San Juan Island. The bartender overheard the man spouting off to his friends that he had inside information no one else had. The sheriff went to talk to the guy, who totally clammed up. Finn and a couple of the other deputies have tried as well, with no luck whatsoever. Cody offered to give it a try, and Finn decided that it couldn't hurt, so Cody headed over on the first ferry this morning."

"It sounds like the same guy is responsible for all the missing women. Given that, it seems like it would be easy to catch up with him. I assume the guy is bringing these women over on the ferry."

"Finn isn't sure," I informed her. "Based on what Finn has been told, some random guy seems to be meeting women in a bar somewhere in Seattle. He enters into a conversation with them, and then at some point, he invites them to spend the weekend with him in the islands. Finn isn't sure if the guy brings them to the islands and then does whatever it is he's been doing with these women, or if he simply uses the trip to lure them into his car."

"It's been months. It seems like the sheriff would know more."

"Finn told me that when the first woman went missing, no one took it all that seriously. The missing woman's best friend didn't even file a report until her friend had been missing for several days, and even then, she filed it in Seattle, where both she and the missing person live. She told the officer who took the report that her friend had called her on Friday of the previous week and told her that she met a totally awesome guy who had invited her on a weekend getaway to the San Juan Islands. She assured the friend she'd be back for work on Monday. When she didn't return on Monday, the friend assumed the woman was simply having a wonderful time and had extended her trip. I guess the missing woman was prone to spontaneous acts such as dropping everything to head out of town with some random guy she just met. The woman who filed the report said that her friend probably wouldn't have even called her, but they had plans on Saturday, which she needed to cancel."

"So this woman meets this guy in a bar who offers to bring her to the islands for a romantic getaway, and she goes with him despite the fact she just met him?" Tara asked.

"According to what the friend who filed the missing persons report told the officer who took her statement."

"Okay. So the friend of this spontaneous woman wasn't too worried when the friend doesn't show up on Monday as planned but begins to become concerned when she's not back by Tuesday?"

I nodded. "According to Finn, who has a copy of the missing persons report and has spoken to the officer who took it, the friend tried calling the missing woman's cell when she didn't show up for work on Tuesday. She continued to call and leave messages over the course of the day Tuesday and into Wednesday. When the missing woman still hadn't called her back or shown up for work, she decided to file the missing persons report. Finn said that at this point, the officer on duty filed the report but wasn't overly worried. The missing woman had, after all, been a twenty-four-year-old single party-girl who had a reputation for doing this sort of thing. I'm not sure why the officer even forwarded the report to the local sheriff other than the woman who filed the report did say that her friend specifically mentioned that this man she'd just met planned to take her to the San Juan Islands. It wasn't until the same officer received another missing persons report almost four weeks later that he even paid much attention to the first report."

"The second missing woman was coming to the islands as well?" Tara asked.

"According to Finn, she was, and also according to Finn, the details were pretty much exactly the same. Some guy in a bar picked up a woman in her twenties and invited her to the islands for the weekend. She called her sister to cancel the plans the two had made for the weekend before taking off with this guy. The sister asked for his name, which the missing person refused to give. The woman never returned to Seattle and her old life, so the sister filed a missing persons report."

"That's actually pretty terrifying," Tara said. "Danny said Finn found out about a third missing person just last week."

I nodded. "Exact same story. Woman goes to bar, meets man who invites her to the islands for the weekend, woman calls friend to cancel plans, woman is never seen again. I think, however, the really frightening part of this is that Finn has absolutely no idea how many women are actually missing. He knows about these three because the women called someone and told them they were coming to the islands with some guy they just met. But there could be other victims who didn't call anyone before they simply left with the guy, so no one knows something might have happened to them. Or there could be other women who did call someone to let them know they were going out of town but didn't mention their intent to head to the islands, so our sheriff didn't get a heads up."

"So, are you saying there could be dozens of missing women?" Tara asked.

I shrugged. "I really don't know and can't know for certain, but it does seem to me that it is likely there are more than three. I know the sheriff is working with the Seattle PD to go back through all their missing persons cases involving women in their twenties for the past six months."

"That sounds like a lot of data to go through."

"It is, but the Seattle PD has some pretty upscale computer software that can do much of the searching for them."

"And what will they do once they have a list?" Tara asked.

I frowned. "I'm not sure. I guess Finn will get photos of the missing women and start asking around. If they were in the area, someone must have seen them."

"Maybe we should volunteer to help out," Tara suggested. "Maybe get the Scooby gang together."

"Yeah, that might be a good idea. I'll call Finn and ask about it."

"Call Finn, and if he wants to meet, why don't you, Cody, Finn, and Siobhan come by the bar this evening. Maybe your mom can babysit Connor," she referred to Finn and Siobhan's son. "We can share some nachos and a pitcher of beer. It's been a while since we all hung out, and since the bar has been pretty dead, we should be able to snag a booth out of the way and talk about how we can help Finn."

"If we come to O'Malley's, will you and Danny be able to get away?" I asked.

"I think so. Cassie will be there to cover the bar and, like I said, it's been pretty dead during the week. If it's too crowded to chat, we can all head to Finn and Siobhan's after we close. Not only are we closed on Sundays and Mondays, but we're closing at eight on weekdays until the summer tourist season hits."

"Okay," I said. "I'll check with Cody, Finn, and Siobhan, and let you know."

Chatting with Tara had helped me to forget about the knot in my stomach for a short period of time, but by the time I'd paid for our lunch and set out toward the newspaper Cody and I owned, that old familiar feeling had returned. My anxiety had been building for days, and I really had no idea what the source of that anxiety might be. No, I didn't think I was anxious about the missing women. For all I knew, this man used a weekend on the islands as a lure but never left Seattle. And yes, it had shaken me to the core when the bookstore Tara and I had poured so much of ourselves into had been destroyed, but that had been months ago, and I'd had time to adjust to the loss. And I supposed there had been a period of adjustment when I'd moved out of my cabin and into the mansion where I now lived with Cody and our good friend, Mr. Parsons, but even that seemed to feel a bit more natural by this point. While I did miss the intimacy of my cabin, I found that I very much liked having breakfast with Mr. Parsons every morning. Not only was he a lot more cheerful since Cody and I moved in full-time, but he seemed to go out of his way to make sure I was happy as well. He even allowed me to help him with whichever crossword puzzle he was working on, which was something he'd never allowed anyone else to do.

When I arrived at the newspaper on foot, I found the front door unlocked. I didn't see Cody's truck, but he sometimes parked in the alley behind the building and entered through the back door. I entered the building and tossed the small backpack I used as a purse on the counter, calling out his name. When he didn't answer, I called out again. "Cody, are you here?" I headed down the short hallway toward the office at the back of the building. It was empty. "Cody," I called again, heading toward the room known as the morgue where we kept copies of all the old newspapers. We had a copy of every newspaper ever printed since the *Madrona Island News* was established more than twenty-five years ago. "Cody," I said, pushing the door open.

I'm really not sure what happened after that. I remembered that I'd stuck my head in the door, felt something slam into me from behind, and when I woke up, there was a filthy rag stuffed into my mouth. If that wasn't bad enough, someone had also tied my arms and legs to a chair with a thick rope. My first instinct was to scream, which I tried doing, although nothing other than a sort of moan came out. I then tried to pull my arms and legs free, but whoever had tied me up had done a heck of a good job. My head was killing me, but otherwise, I seemed to be fine. I looked down at my chest and lap, which was all I could really see from my position and didn't notice any blood.

Who on earth had done this to me?

I took a deep breath in through my nose since I couldn't breathe through my mouth. *Okay, Cait*, I said to myself. *Just breathe.*

The urge to panic was great, but I knew I needed to keep my head if I was going to get out of this alive. I had no idea how long I'd been unconscious. The morgue had no windows, so I couldn't even see out to gauge the time of day. I knew Cody planned to be back at some point this afternoon, although I had no idea how long his interview might have taken or which ferry he might have managed to catch for his return to the island. I didn't think whoever had done this to me was still in the building, but I couldn't be sure. I forced myself to relax and listen. At first, I didn't hear anything. I figured I was safe until I heard a crash coming from the other room.

Oh, God! I squeezed my eyes close and said a little prayer.

When I opened my eyes, a white cat with a dark tail, dark ears, and a dark mask stood at the doorway, looking inside. I hoped it was the cat and not the man who tied me up who'd caused the crash I'd heard. I tried to call the cat over, although I really had no idea what good that would do since cats couldn't actually untie ropes, but with the gag in my mouth, all that came out were grunts.

"Meow," the cat said, wandering further into the room.

Please, please, please be a Tansy cat.

I looked directly at the cat. I couldn't speak, but if my witchy friend, Tansy, had sent this cat, I knew he or she would and could figure out a way to help me.

Hoping the cat could read my thoughts, I began to mentally beg for it to go and get help. *Find Finn,* I screamed in my mind.

"Meow," the cat said before turning and trotting back out the door.

Once the cat left, I tried listening again, hoping against hope that the person who'd knocked me out was long gone. I began to relax a bit when all I heard was silence. If the person who'd tied me up had left, I figured I'd be fine. I didn't appear to be hurt, so all I really needed to do was wait. Of course, waiting patiently for a cat I didn't even know for certain was a Tansy cat to go and get help wasn't really all that easy with a gag in my mouth and a stiff rope cutting into my wrists, so I took several deep breaths in through my nose and tried to think about something else.

My mind raced from subject to subject, unable to really settle on anything until I hit upon the concept of why. Why had someone broken in here in the first place? It wasn't like we had anything of value. We didn't have cash on hand, nor did we store valuable antiques or precious gems. This building was currently used to print the weekly newspaper and prepare it for distribution. Old editions of the newspaper were stored in the room in which I was tied, and the printing press was of some value I supposed, but it certainly wasn't the sort of thing one would break in and steal. Cody had files and a computer in his office, but again, nothing of value. The idea that anyone would break into this building made absolutely no sense, no matter how I looked at it.

After the cat had been gone for at least fifteen minutes, I began to grow antsy once again. I tried wiggling my wrists to loosen the rope, but all that did was tear the skin under the ropes. I was fine, I assured myself. I just needed to wait. Either the cat would return with help, or Cody would come back and find me. *It's fine*, I said to myself over and over again, figuring that I might eventually begin to believe the lie I was telling myself.

The urge to thrash around was great, so I looked around the room, hoping to find something to focus on other than the panic in my gut. Having a total meltdown wasn't going to help me in the least, and, in the end, thrashing around might actually hurt me. I wished the room had windows, so I had something other than shelves and shelves of old newspapers to look at. A man named Orson Cobalter had established the newspaper. When Orson decided to move to Florida to be near his family, he put the business he'd run for most of his life up for sale. Cody had just returned to the island after leaving the Navy, and on somewhat of a whim, he'd decided to buy it. Orson had been old school and hadn't updated for a quarter of a century, so Cody had needed to put a ton of money, and even more labor, into the place. But he'd eventually modernized it to the point where he had a highly respected weekly publication. Between the two of us, Cody and I were able to eke out a comfortable living, doing work we felt was both important and worthwhile. Really what more could anyone ask for?

Still, there wasn't a single thing in this building that, in my mind, would warrant a break-in. No matter how many times I mentally inventoried every item in the place, I still couldn't come up with a single motive for anyone to have done what they had.

"Cody," Finn called out.

Thank God.

I tried to yell, but all I came up with was a groan. I waited while Finn made his way through the building, calling out Cody's name.

"Cait! Oh, my God, what happened?"

I glanced down at the gag in my mouth as a way of letting him know that if he wanted me to answer that question, he was going to have to remove the gag. He hurried forward and did just that.

"How'd you find me?" I asked as he worked on the ropes around my wrists and ankles.

"This stray cat showed up at the front door of the sheriff's office, having a total freak out. I opened the door to see if I could figure out what her problem was, which is when she took off in this direction. After all the years of living around you and your magical cats, I knew I should follow."

I put my hand on my head to check for blood once my wrists were free. "I'm glad you did. Cody would have found me eventually, but I really don't know when he'll be back, and I wasn't all that comfortable waiting."

Finn freed my ankles and then stood up. "Are you hurt? Should I take you to the emergency room?"

I rubbed my wrists as I shook my head. "I'm fine. A little bump on my head, but it isn't bleeding. I just need an aspirin."

"You might have a concussion. I'm taking you to the emergency room. You can tell me what happened on the way."

"The cat," I said. "Where is the cat?"

Finn looked around. "I don't know. Maybe she figured her job was done and went back to wherever it is she came from." Finn took my hand in his. "Do you have a purse or something?"

"My backpack. It's on the front counter. We should call Cody."

"You can call him from the car. Right now, I'm getting you checked out."

"Yes, Dad," I groaned.

Finn and I had been friends for a long time, and I really didn't mind him fussing over me, but I was worried about the cat and wished he'd let me look for her before we left. When he insisted that she was probably fine, I supposed I knew he was most likely right; still, the cat had really come through for me, and I wanted to thank her. Little did I know it at the time, but the cat, whose name I would later learn was Mystique, had just begun her involvement in my life.

Chapter 2

"Caitlin Hart West?" the doctor asked.

"That's me, but you can call me Cait." I forced a smile, although smiling was the last thing I felt like doing. "You must be new to Madrona Island. I've lived here my entire life, and I'm sure we haven't met."

"I am new to the hospital and the island. My name is Doctor Whitmeyer." He looked down at my chart. "I see here that you suffered a blow to the head and were knocked unconscious."

"I was," I confirmed. "But I'm totally fine now. I wouldn't even be here except my overly protective brother-in-law insisted I come in so someone could verify that my brain wasn't scrambled."

He cocked a grin. "I see. Why don't we start by you telling me exactly what happened."

The next ten minutes consisted of him listening to my story, listening to my heart, checking my pupils, and checking for reflexes. He asked me a bunch of questions I assumed were to prove I really hadn't lost my marbles, then he deemed me okay to go home as long as I had someone there with me who could and would keep an eye on me and watch for symptoms associated with a concussion. Cody's trip to San Juan Island had run late, and he was still on the ferry, so Finn promised to take me home with him until my husband arrived to take over babysitting duty. Once we arrived at his house, my big sister, Siobhan, took over, and Finn left to return to the newspaper to meet with the deputy he'd assigned the job of dusting for prints and looking for physical evidence.

"Are you sure you're okay?" Siobhan asked after settling me on the sofa with a cup of tea.

"I'm fine. Really." I lifted a hand to my head. "I do have a brand new lump that wasn't there this morning, but except for a slight headache, I feel fine. Where's Connor?"

"Mom took him to the park. They should be home in an hour or so unless Mom calls and asks to keep him overnight. She's been doing that more and more often lately."

"It's sweet that she and Gabe want to spend so much time with him, and it does give you and Finn some alone time."

"It does, and I'm grateful. I'm also happy that Connor has a chance to really get to know Gammy and Gabe. He adores being with them as much as they seem to adore having him. In fact, Gabe even built a swing set with a treehouse of sorts and a winding slide in their back yard. Of course, Connor is too young to really appreciate the elaborate toy set, but in a year or two, I'm sure we won't be able to get him off it."

"It seems to me that Connor might enjoy the swing set even more if he had a little brother or sister to play with," I hinted.

"Or maybe a cousin," she shot back.

"Or maybe we can help him find a little friend to hang out with." The last thing I wanted to do was to get into a discussion about Cody and I having a baby since adding to our family was not a possibility I even wanted to consider at this point.

"Does Cody know to pick you up here?" Siobhan asked, mercifully changing the subject.

"He does." I glanced at the clock. "He should be here in about twenty minutes. I guess I should call Tara. We had lunch together, and she invited us all to the bar for beer and nachos, but there is no way Cody will want to do that now."

"Let's grab some pizzas, and all have dinner here. What time do Danny, Cassie, and Tara get off?"

"Not until eight," I said. "Aiden went fishing, so there's no one to cover."

"Okay, then maybe you and I and Finn and Cody can have dinner, and the others can meet us here for a drink when they get off."

"That's a good idea. I'll call Tara and suggest it. After what happened today, I'm sure each and every one of my siblings and friends is going to want to count all my fingers and toes and make sure I'm okay."

"I'll call Tara. You just relax."

I laid my head back on the sofa and closed my eyes while Siobhan called the bar to make the arrangements. Cody pulled up while Siobhan was on the phone with our mother arranging for her to keep Connor overnight.

"Are you okay?" Cody asked, hugging me hard enough to push the air from my lungs.

"Except for the fact I can't breathe, I'm fine."

"Sorry." He took a step back. "I can't believe someone broke into the newspaper. We don't have anything of value."

"I know." He sat down beside me, and I laid my head on his shoulder. "I've gone over it again and again in my mind, and I can't think of a single reason for anyone to want to break into that building."

"Is Finn there now?"

I nodded. "They're taking prints, looking for evidence, all the normal stuff. Siobhan is arranging for Mom to keep Connor overnight. We thought the four of us could have dinner after Finn gets back. Maybe he'll have some news by then."

"I hope so." Cody ran a hand through his hair. "I'm going to run home and check on Mr. Parsons. I'll let him know we won't be home for dinner, and take the dogs for a quick walk."

"Okay. I'm fine here with Siobhan to hover over me. Before you go, did you learn anything interesting from the man you went to San Juan Island to speak to?"

"Interesting, yes; relevant, I'm honestly not sure. I'm sure Finn will want to hear what I have to say, so I think I'll wait and go over everything when he gets here."

"Okay. If you see a white cat with a dark tail and dark ears and mask, I think she is a Tansy cat. She's the cat that went and found Finn and persuaded him to come and rescue me. She took off while Finn was untying me, but I have a feeling we have more to do.

If she shows up at the house, please let her in. I don't want her to take off again."

"Okay. I will. Maybe you should call Tansy and see if she can fill you in on the details surrounding the cat. She usually has a name at the very least."

"That's a good idea. I'll do that."

Cody leaned over and kissed me gently on the lips. "I won't be long. Do you need anything?"

"My blue sweatshirt. I think it's going to get cold once the sun goes down."

After Cody left to check on Mr. Parsons, I called Tansy, who informed me that the cat's name was Mystique and that our relationship was indeed only just getting started. Tansy didn't seem concerned that Mystique took off after leading Finn to me, so I decided not to be concerned either. I asked Tansy if she knew what Mystique and I were supposed to do together, and her only reply was that once we figured out what the person who broke into the newspaper was after, the rest of the mystery we were to solve would fall into place. That was a vague answer, but Tansy was always vague, so I supposed I really wasn't expecting much more. Still, given the situation, more would have been nice. I really didn't know if Tansy had information she chose not to share with me, or if her insights came to her in the disjointed way she shared them, but over the years, I had learned to trust both Tansy and the cats that came into our lives, which was exactly what I was going to do at this juncture.

Chapter 3

Cody and Finn arrived at the house at about the same time. It was already after seven at this point, so I called Tara and told her that we would wait for her, Danny, and Cassie to get off if they wanted to join us for pizza. Tara informed me that since the bar was dead, Danny had decided to close early, so they'd be earlier than expected.

"So, where do we even start?" Cassie asked once we'd all served ourselves and had gathered around the table. "Do we start with what happened to Cait, Cody's trip to San Juan Island, or the status of Finn's investigation to date into both cases?"

"We need to start with what happened to Cait," Tara said. "Tell me everything that happened from the time you left me at the café until Finn found you at the newspaper."

"It's a short story," I responded. "When I walked to the newspaper and found the front door unlocked, I figured Cody was back from San Juan Island. His truck wasn't in the street, but he does occasionally park in the alley in the back, so I just assumed that was what he'd done. I called out his name, and when he didn't answer, I walked down the hallway. I poked my head in the office and found it empty, so I poked my head in the morgue, felt a presence behind me and then pressure, like something or someone slamming into me, and when I regained consciousness, I was tied to a chair with a filthy rag in my mouth."

"That must have been horrifying," Tara gasped.

"It wasn't fun."

"How long were you there before Finn found you?" Danny asked.

I lifted a shoulder. "I'm not sure. Probably not all that long. When I came to, I struggled to get away, but all that did was chew up my wrists. I heard a crash and thought it was the person who tied me up, but it was a cat, who I've since learned is named Mystique. I couldn't speak to the cat due to the gag, but I mentally begged for her to go and get Finn, and she did." I frowned. "I wonder how she got in. I'm sure I closed the front door when I came in, and I didn't notice the back door being open."

"Maybe she slipped in when whoever broke in came in," Finn said.

I supposed it could have happened that way. "Anyway, after Finn rescued me, he took me to the hospital to have my head checked out, and then I came here to let my big sister fuss over me."

"It's a good thing this person just tied you up and didn't really hurt you," Danny said.

Cody looked at Finn. "Do we have anything we can use to identify the person who did this? Prints? Fibers? Anything?"

Finn shook his head. "There were a lot of different prints on the front door, but the newspaper is the sort of place a lot of folks visit. We focused on your office and the morgue, but so far, we've only been able to identify prints belonging to you and Cait. As for other physical evidence, there doesn't appear to be any, but I do plan to have the guys go over everything again. I think our best chance of discovering who broke in is to figure out what they took, assuming they took anything."

"I'll take a look around in the morning," Cody said.

"There really isn't anything to take," I added. "Unless someone was after an old newspaper for some reason."

"Why would anyone want an old newspaper?" Tara asked.

"Maybe they wanted information provided in one of the older editions," I added.

"Isn't all of that available online?" Tara asked.

Cody joined in. "No. Orson didn't digitize anything. When I bought the place, the first thing I did was modernize so that every edition is available in both a physical format and a digital format. I've been meaning to go back and digitize the back copies, but so far, I haven't had the time to do so or the funds to hire someone to do it."

"So maybe someone wanted information provided in one of the newspapers printed before you bought the place," Danny said.

"That does make the most sense," I said.

"How can we figure out which one?" Siobhan asked.

Cody answered. "We'll need to go through the stacks and stacks of newspapers we have and see which, if any, are missing. As far as I know, there was one copy of every edition ever published in the morgue, although we have two copies of the more recent editions. It will be time consuming but doable."

"What if the person who broke in didn't take the newspaper they were after?" Danny asked. "What if he or she simply found what they were looking for and took a photo of it? Or what if we're wrong, and the goal was not to steal a newspaper but to do something else? Take something else?"

"Then figuring out why whoever broke in did so is going to be nearly impossible unless Finn is able to find some physical evidence," Cody said.

The room fell into silence. The idea that there was someone out there who'd wanted something inside the newspaper office, which they may or may have gotten before I interrupted them, left me with a feeling of trepidation. If they hadn't found what they were after, would they try again?

"So, how did your interview go?" I asked Cody, deciding that we'd hashed out the "who broke into the newspaper" question to the extent we could at this point.

"It went okay, but I'm not sure if what I've learned will help Finn," Cody answered as he looked toward Finn. "I spoke to the bartender at the Yellow Feather as you suggested, and he eventually admitted that a man had been in the bar a few weeks ago who was bragging about having information relating to another man he knew who supposedly picked women up in Seattle and brought them to the islands. It took a bit of persuasion, but I was ultimately able to convince the bartender to steer me toward the man, who, as it turns out, works in the marina at Friday Harbor. I went to the marina to speak to the man the bartender steered me toward. Initially, he was reluctant to share any information, so I offered to buy him a drink, and after a few shots, I was finally able to ascertain that the man, whose name was Pete, had overheard another patron sitting nearby bragging that he had picked up women on the mainland and brought them to the islands for some unconventional fun. I asked Pete if he knew what the guy meant by unconventional fun, and he just grinned but didn't elaborate. To be honest, I'm not even sure he knows what the guy meant, but I did learn that the name of the man who'd been bragging about picking up women was Jack. I also got a general description of the man going by the name Jack, although I doubt six feet tall, brown hair, brown eyes, and average build will be particularly helpful. I asked Pete about meeting with a sketch artist, but he refused, saying he really didn't remember what the guy looked like beyond a general description."

"Anything else?" Finn asked.

"While I was at the bar, I'd asked the bartender if there had been a cocktail waitress working that night, and he said there had been and gave me her name. I went back to the bar to talk to the woman who told me her name was Veronica. I described the man with dark hair Pete had referred to, and she said that she remembered the guy. I asked her for a description, which was very similar to the description Pete gave, but she added that the guy had scratch marks on his face, which she asked about. He simply winked and told her that things had gotten a little rough with his date the previous weekend. She also noticed that he had an injury on the palm of his right hand. She thought it looked like a rope burn. When she asked about it, he told her that he'd been careless while sailing. I suppose it could have happened that way."

"Or he might have received the rope burn while strangling his date," Tara added.

"I suppose that explanation works as well," Cody admitted. "Veronica also directed me to another regular bar patron named David, who also works at a marina, although David works at Roche Harbor, whereas Pete works at Friday Harbor. David initially seemed unwilling to talk to me, so, like I had with Pete, I offered to buy him a drink and somewhere around his third shot of whiskey, he admitted that he'd also seen this man, who he confirmed goes by the name Jack, at the Yellow Feather. He also added that he'd seen the same man in other bars in the area, including a bar on Orcas Island and a bar here on Madrona Island."

"Our bar?" Danny asked.

"No. A bar on the north shore. Anyway, according to David, Jack is the sort to brag about all the women he's bagged in recent months, but David suspected he was lying since, while he'd run into him four or five times in the past several months, he'd always been alone. I'm not sure how this information is going to help us track down the man or the missing women, but I suppose it's a start."

"Maybe this Jack wasn't lying about the sailing," I said. "Maybe he did burn his hand while he was out on his boat. I guess we can check with marinas in the area. Maybe someone knows a customer named Jack who fits the general description of the man."

"I'll take care of that," Finn said. "Anything else?"

"No, not really," Cody answered. "The bartender I spoke to did say that he'd never seen the guy before that night and hadn't seen him since. David said he had seen him in the bar a few times, but I suppose the place has more than one bartender. Either that or the bartender was lying for some reason. If David had indeed seen this guy on Orcas Island and Madrona Island as well as San Juan Island, it seems he's moving between the islands rather than staying in one place. If he's bringing women to the islands to kill them, maybe he moves around so he won't draw attention to himself. He may even have a home on one of the small private islands in the area."

"So, what exactly is the theory here?" Siobhan asked. "Are we saying that some guy picks up women in Seattle and brings them to the islands for a weekend of sexcapades before he kills them and dumps their bodies?"

"That's the theory at this point," Finn said. "The theory is based purely on the fact that three women went missing from Seattle bars who called and spoke to a friend or family member, letting them know they'd met a guy who was bringing them to the islands, and they were never seen again. We don't know if there were others. There very well might be. The three missing women linked to the islands are only linked because they called someone before they left and specifically mentioned coming to the islands. For all we know, this guy might have been picking up women every weekend for months and months."

"It's also possible that the guy who picked up these women in Seattle bars and promised them a trip to the islands never left Seattle with them," I added.

"Cait's right," Finn said. "At this point, I'm just trying to dig up some sort of proof to support the theory that there actually is a serial killer out there using Seattle bars as his hunting ground and the San Juan Islands as his killing place. I'm afraid all I really have is a theory, and unless I can find more, a theory may be all we ever have."

"Has the FBI been notified?" Danny asked.

"The Seattle PD has been in contact with someone from the FBI. I'm not sure if they've been able to make enough of a case to get their attention, but they do know what we suspect."

"Can we help?" I asked Finn.

"No. At this point, I'm just trying to find anyone who might know anything that will support the theory I've been working off since I was made aware of the most recent missing woman."

"Is the Seattle PD going back through their missing persons cases to look for other possible matches?" I asked.

"They have someone on it. The three women we know of who called and told a friend or family member they'd met a man and were coming to the islands all called on a Friday and indicated they met the man at a bar, but the three women had been at different bars. All the women were in their twenties with a propensity to do things such as taking off with men they just met. I think the Seattle PD is looking for other missing women who fit that general profile even if they hadn't called anyone before leaving with the guy who'd picked them up."

"What about questioning the bartenders and cocktail waitresses working in the bars the women went missing from?" Tara asked.

"That's being taken care of by the Seattle PD as well. We've been sharing information, so I assume they'll let me know if they come up with anything. I'll call and talk to my contact tomorrow about Cody's conversation with the bartender and cocktail waitress from the Yellow Feather. All we can really do at this point is to keep digging and see where it takes us."

Chapter 4

Thursday, April 2

Cody and I went through all the back issues of the newspaper Thursday morning to verify that none were missing. I was happy that we still had all the back issues since most were probably irreplaceable, but we still had no idea why someone had broken in. We'd gone through everything again and had determined that not a single thing, as far as we could tell, was missing. Cody did say that it looked as if someone had gone through the files in his file cabinet, so I supposed I might have interrupted the intruder before he'd had a chance to do whatever it was that he had planned to do. If that was the case, would he try again? Neither Cody nor Finn had a feel for what the intruder who'd tied me up would do next, but both men had decided that we needed to beef up our security system with an alarm and sturdier locks for the windows and doors.

Mystique still hadn't shown up, which had me somewhat worried. I'd stopped by Herbalities to speak to Tansy on my way to the newspaper this morning, and she'd simply said that the cat would appear when she was needed. I knew she was right. That was how it had worked in the past. I wasn't certain why I had so much anxiety this time around, but maybe the problem was simply my general feeling of anxiety getting all mixed up with my concern about the missing cat.

There are those who would say that I was anxious because of what happened to me, but truth be told, I'd been anxious before I'd been knocked out and tied up. Of course, being assaulted hadn't helped. In fact, at this point, my anxiety was bordering on paranoia, which was not a feeling I welcomed. A part of me seemed to know that something bad was going to happen, but since I couldn't give words to that premonition, I experienced this dread as undefined anxiety. This may sound strange, but I honestly felt that I'd feel safer once the cat appeared, and I knew that help was close at hand.

"Tara called me this morning," I said to Cody as we took a break to have lunch. "She's meeting with a representative of the insurance company at one-thirty and asked if I could attend."

"I take it the meeting is here on the island?"

I nodded. "The meeting is on the wharf in front of Coffee Cat Books. The guy wants to take some additional photos and says he has more questions for us."

"Haven't they already done that more than once?" Cody asked.

"They have, but I guess they are doing it again. Personally, I think they're stalling, but what can we do other than comply with their wishes and hope that eventually this all gets figured out."

Cody took a bite of his sandwich. "The thing that seems the strangest to me is that Coffee Cat Books not only carried property insurance but a loss of income policy as well. You'd think the insurance company would be as anxious to get the store open as you are so they can close the claim as quickly as possible."

"You'd think. I really don't know why they are dragging their feet the way they are."

"Maybe the guy you meet with today will be able to fill in some of the blanks or at least answer some of your questions." Cody grabbed his cola and took a sip.

"I hope so." I leaned a hip against a counter. My appetite was pretty much non-existent, so I made due by picking at a bag of potato chips I wasn't really eating. "I thought Tara would be experiencing out of control anxiety at this point, but she seems perfectly happy working at the bar with Danny. I'm the one who can't quite seem to get a handle on things, and I really don't know why. I'm not usually the anxious sort."

Cody got up from where he was sitting, crossed the room, and gave me a hug. "You've had a lot of changes in your life in the past few months. You're bound to feel some anxiety at this point. Just know that if you need a hug or you need to talk, I'm here for you."

I hugged Cody tighter. "I know, and that helps more than you know."

Tara was waiting for me at the wharf when I arrived. I noticed two men who I assumed were from the insurance company, standing off to the side having a discussion.

"So, what's going on?" I asked Tara.

"I'm not sure. When the men first arrived, one of them went inside for about thirty minutes. When he came out, he spoke to the man in the blue sweater who then made a call. Shortly after that, the man in the plaid shirt showed up, and the two men have been chatting ever since."

"Based on their expressions, it seems they are having a serious conversation."

Tara bit her lower lip. "Yeah. I'm not sure what's up, but I'm not liking the way this is going."

Shortly after I arrived, the man in the plaid shirt left, and the man in the blue sweater approached Tara and me.

"Thank you both for meeting me here," the man said.

"We were happy to. What's going on?" Tara asked.

I could hear the fear in her voice, so I grabbed her hand in a show of solidarity.

"We've done some research and found out that there is an ordinance on your island that requires any structure undergoing a remodel or addition compromising greater than forty percent of the total square footage be brought completely up to code. The building you purchased to house Coffee Cat Books is a very old building that will need a lot of work to bring it current, and given the nature of the structural damage, reworking less than forty percent is an unrealistic number to shoot for. The insurance company has determined that it would be more cost-effective to simply label the building as a tear down rather than to repair it."

Tara paled. "What does that mean?"

"That means that per your policy, your settlement will be a percentage of the appraised value of the building."

"So, you aren't going to pay for the building to be repaired?" I verified.

"We are not. You will get a lump sum settlement that you can use however you want. If you want to try to repair the building, the decision is yours, but I wouldn't recommend doing that. The cannery you remodeled when you opened the bookstore was already an old building, and the damage from the explosion is substantial. Additionally, given the fact that the structure was built on a wharf, it has been subjected to a lot of movement over the years. I'm afraid when you add the damage caused by the explosion to the damage that already existed, repair really isn't a viable option."

"How much in dollars are we talking about?" Tara asked.

"I estimate it will cost you more than double the settlement you will receive to repair the place. My recommendation is that you use your settlement to pay off your loan, demolish the building, and settle your debts."

Tara squeezed my hand hard enough that it hurt, but while I flinched, I didn't pull away. "So, you're saying that we are out of business."

"I'm afraid that would appear to be the case." The man handed Tara a piece of paper. "The total dollar amount of your settlement is being calculated as we speak. Someone will call you next week to go over the details."

Tara looked down at the document, which I imagined explained in writing what the man had just told us. "Once we're paid off, we can choose what we want to do with the property," she verified.

"Yes. You can choose what to do. Your loan from the bank will most likely be due upon receipt of the settlement, and I honestly don't think you'll have a lot left to do repairs or to rebuild the property after that, but I suppose you can try to get funding from another source, that's up to you." He held out his hand and shook each of ours. "I really am very sorry."

With that, he walked away.

I looked at Tara. "What are we going to do?"

"I don't know," she whispered as a tear slid down her cheek.

"Let's head to the bar. We can talk this through," I suggested. "I'll call Cody and see if he can meet us there."

She nodded but didn't speak. I had to wonder if this was the unseen disaster I'd been stressing over as of late, but somehow I didn't think so. In fact, based on the pit in my gut, I was pretty sure that things were only going to go downhill from here.

I was happy to see that the bar was deserted when Tara and I walked in. During the summer, the place was packed open to close, but during the winter and early spring, there was a definite lunch crowd followed by a midafternoon lull, which led into the early evening hours when the after-work and dinner crowds would come in. I figured we had two hours before the happy hour group started to congregate.

"So, how'd it go?" Danny asked.

"Not good," Tara said, a tone of defeat in her voice.

"What happened?" he asked, pulling her into his arms.

Tara started to explain but ended up sobbing, so I took over and caught him up to date the best I could.

"Where's Cassie?" I asked once I'd filled Danny in.

"She's on a break until four," Danny answered.

"I called Cody, and he'll be here as soon as he finishes what he's working on," I informed the others. "I'm hoping that between the four of us, we can come up with a plan that will allow us to repair the bookstore rather than razing it."

"Maybe we should call Siobhan and get her input on the code issue," Danny said. "If she doesn't have the answers we need, she'll have direct access to whoever does."

"That's a good idea." As mayor, Siobhan would understand the options available to us.

Once Cody and Siobhan showed up, the five of us sat down and went over things. Tara and I shared what the man from the insurance company had told us while Siobhan looked over the document he'd given to Tara.

"It is true that about three years ago, the island council voted to enact certain building guidelines meant to improve the quality of the infrastructure on the island," Siobhan started. "The existing infrastructure was grandfathered in, but all new construction was mandated to comply with the new guidelines. As for existing buildings, it was determined that in the case of remodeling or additions, if the affected area was greater than forty percent of the total square footage, then upgrades which would bring the entire structure into compliance would be mandated in order to obtain a permit."

"So the guy from the insurance company was probably right," Tara said. "It would cost a lot more to repair the building than to tear it down and start over."

"That's not technically true," Siobhan said. "But it would cost the insurance more to make the needed repairs and upgrades than to total the building and pay you the appraised value minus any deductibles you may have."

"So, what do we do?" Tara asked.

"I'm not sure at this point," Siobhan said. "Tearing the building down and rebuilding from scratch is going to be costly. I suppose the first thing you'll need to do is speak to the bank and find out what they are willing to do."

"I can do that," Tara said. "I'll call them today and make an appointment to speak to someone."

"And I have a couple of buddies who are contractors," Danny said. "I'll see if they'd do a rough workup of costs to rebuild. It won't be exact at this point, but we should be able to get a number to shoot for."

I couldn't help but notice the look of adoration Tara sent Danny. Oh yeah, things were definitely back on.

"I guess we should bring both Cassie and Willow up to speed," I said. "I know Cassie will be at the bar later, but I'll call Willow and explain the situation." Willow was our part-time employee.

"What are we going to do if the bank won't give us a loan to rebuild?" Tara asked.

"I don't know," I admitted. "I guess for now all we can do is gather all the facts and all the numbers, and then take it from there."

The five of us spoke a while longer, and then Cody and I headed back toward the newspaper. He had some work he needed to finish up before we left for the day. I had to admit I was having a hard time really grasping the situation. From the moment the bookstore had blown up, I'd just assumed that we'd repair it and get on with our lives. Never once had I considered that Coffee Cat Books might be gone for good.

"It's going to be okay," Cody said, pulling me into his arms once we'd arrived at his truck. "We'll figure something out."

"I know. I'm not worried." I paused. "Well, I guess that isn't true. I am worried, but it's early, and I know we really have no reason to give up hope. I just feel bad for Tara. Coffee Cat Books was our joint idea, but it has always been her baby. She's the one who put the most work into it. She's the one who made it successful. I actually love coming to work with you at the newspaper, probably even more than I enjoyed working at the bookstore, but Tara doesn't have anything to fall back on the way I do."

"She seems to have Danny," Cody pointed out.

I nodded. "Yes. She seems to have Danny. At least for today. But given their past..."

"Yeah," Cody said. "I know what you're saying." He opened the door to the truck and helped me in before going around to the driver's side. "Whatever happens with the loan, we'll make sure Tara is okay," Cody said. "She's family, and family takes care of their own."

Chapter 5

I called Willow as we drove back toward the newspaper. She lived with a man named Alex Turner who was the son of a very rich man named Balthazar Pottage, so she wasn't worried about the loss of income, but she did say that she missed Tara and me, and she really missed hanging out at the bookstore three days a week. I promised we'd do a better job of getting together for lunch every single week and then encouraged her to hang in there.

Cody pulled up in front of the newspaper, and we both got out. I was the first to arrive at the front door. I expected it to be locked and was surprised to find it open.

"Cody, did you forget to lock the door?" I asked.

"No. I specifically remember checking the doors and windows before I left."

"Well, it's unlocked." I looked at the local sheriff's office next door, which is where Finn kept an office. "I think we should get Finn. The last time I found the door open and went in anyway, it didn't turn out so well."

"Yeah," Cody said. "I agree that we should get Finn before going in, but I don't see his car. Let's check his office. If he isn't there, we'll wait in the truck until he can get back here."

As it turned out, Finn wasn't in his office, but he was only about ten minutes away. He told us not to go in and to wait in the truck, which we already planned to do. Cody had ordered an alarm and upgraded security system for the newspaper, but we were weeks away from anyone being able to install it. If these break-ins were going to continue, however, I guess we'd need to find someone who could do it sooner.

Finn pulled up on the street behind us. He pulled out his gun, told us to wait, and then went inside. He came out a few minutes later and told us the coast was clear. He gave us each a pair of gloves, and then the three of us went inside to see what was missing.

Cody and I slowly walked through each room, opening drawers and cupboards. We checked the computers and files and did a brief examination of the newspapers in the morgue.

"I don't see anything missing," Cody said after we'd walked through the entire building.

"Are you sure?" Finn asked.

"As sure as I can be without more time to go through everything," Cody said.

"Why would someone break in here not once but twice and not take anything?" Finn asked.

"I have no idea," Cody admitted. "Cait and I can take a better look around later, but based on a cursory investigation, I really don't see a single thing missing."

Finn went to the door and looked at the lock. "We really do need to get your security system upgraded."

"I have a guy coming by to do just that, but he couldn't come for a few weeks. I guess we can add deadlocks to the doors in the meantime."

"I think that is a must at the very least." Finn looked around. "This isn't a hard lock to pick, and this isn't a busy street. Both times the newspaper was broken into, the newspaper and my office next door were empty. The building that used to house the post office is empty as well now that the post office moved, so I can see how someone would be able to get in without being seen, but again, I'm back to why."

"I have no idea," Cody said.

Finn picked up his cell and made a call. After he hung up, he looked at Cody and me. "I've got someone coming over to dust for prints. The two of you may as well go on home. We'll be working in here for at least several hours."

Cody grabbed his laptop and some files he needed, then the two of us headed back toward Mr. Parsons' house. When we arrived, I found Mystique sitting on the front step.

"I'm so glad you showed up," I said, picking the cat up and scratching her beneath the chin. "I was worried about you."

"Meow."

When I opened the front door, my dog, Max, and Mr. Parsons' dog, Rambler, greeted us. Mystique didn't seem frightened by the dogs. She glanced at them with a look of superior disdain and then basically ignored them. Once we were safely inside, I set her down. She continued to ignore the dogs as she trotted down the hallway like she owned the place.

"Who do we have here?" Mr. Parsons asked when I entered the room. Mystique was already settled onto his lap, and both cat and homeowner looked content.

"That's Mystique. She's the cat who found Finn for me when I was tied up."

"Well, thank you very much, little lady." Mystique looked thrilled to have Mr. Parsons' attention. "She is, of course, welcome to stay as long as she wants, but I'm afraid I don't have supplies for a cat."

"I'll go next door and get everything we need," I offered.

Finn and Siobhan, as well as my younger sister, Cassie, lived on the adjoining estate, which was also home to the Harthaven Cat Sanctuary. When I'd lived in the cabin currently occupied by Cassie, I'd always had cat supplies on hand, but we hadn't had any visiting cats since Cody and I had moved in full-time with Mr. Parsons, so I hadn't brought anything over yet.

"This little lady and I are happy to hang out together while you get what you need," Mr. Parsons offered.

I decided to walk next door to get a cat box, a small bag of litter, and a small bag of cat food. If I needed additional supplies, I could get them later. As I entered the cat sanctuary, I was greeted by some of the current residents. The sanctuary was founded by my Aunt Maggie after the mayor at the time, Mayor Bradley, pushed through a law that made it legal for residents to use any means necessary to remove feral cats from their property. Mayor Bradley hated the island's feral cats, and I think he hoped the residents would join him in his campaign to exterminate the felines, but Maggie had another idea and provided the residents with a humane option.

Initially, the cat sanctuary was full to capacity with both those cats who were deemed untamable and would need to be lifelong residents and those cats who were strays but had the potential to be rehabilitated and rehomed. I spent a lot of time taking those we hoped to find homes for to clinics in Seattle until the cat lounge in Coffee Cat Books opened, providing us a much easier way to showcase the cats.

Additionally, since the inception of the cat sanctuary, Mayor Bradley had passed away, and Siobhan had taken over as mayor. She'd repealed the laws enacted by Bradley, which put safeguards for the feral cats on the island back into place. Now that the cats were once again protected, most of the cats roamed the island freely, some cats just couldn't seem to coexist with humans, so the sanctuary continued to play a vital role for those cats who became a nuisance and needed to find a home.

As of the time of the bombing, the cat sanctuary had been empty except for those cats we'd deemed lifelong residents. I was actually importing cats and kittens from other shelters to feature in the lounge until the moment a madman decided to end everything.

I knew that without the cat lounge to drive adoptions, the sanctuary would eventually fill back up, and I'd be back to transporting cats to Seattle to find homes. I supposed in my mind, reopening the cat lounge was an even more urgent need than reopening the bookstore.

Once I had greeted all the cats and cuddled those who would let me, I took my supplies and headed back to Mr. Parsons' house. I set up the cat box in the laundry room Cody and I shared with Mr. Parsons. I also made sure Mystique had free access to the entire house so she could visit with Mr. Parsons and have access to her cat box, food, and water. Then I grabbed both dogs and set out for a long run, which I hoped would chase away the anxiety that was continuing to build in the back of my mind.

Running had always been my escape; my release from the stressors in my life. I'd been a runner since I was a teen and supposed I'd continue to be one until I was no longer physically able. I was lucky to have a beautiful beach and gently rolling waves as my companion as I settled into a steady rhythm with the dogs running side by side just in front of me.

I took several deep breaths and tried to focus my mind. I still wasn't sure exactly what it was that had me the most bothered. I supposed that I did have reason to be stressed given the fact that I'd been knocked unconscious and tied to a chair, and I'd found out that the bookstore and cat lounge Tara and I had built with pure grit and determination might not be reopened as I'd expected, but I felt that my anxiety was related to something other than either of those events.

I glanced down at my feet as they made contact with the damp sand. Left, right, left, right, I thought to myself as I tried to quiet my mind. It was a beautiful sunny day. The seagulls were milling around, looking for an afternoon snack as an eagle sat in a nearby tree, watching everything that was going on. The waves gently rolled to the shore, barely causing a ripple. I used to love to sit on the deck of my cabin and watch the sea as it changed its mood and tempo with the tide. I supposed part of my emotional duress could be because of my change in residence, which had brought with it a change in everyday patterns and habits. Cody had offered to build me a small cottage with a deck on Mr. Parsons' property where I could watch the sunrises and sunsets and listen to the steady rhythm of the waves. Maybe a small cottage at our new residence wasn't all that bad an idea. Our apartment in the mansion was really gorgeous, but somehow, with the house set back from the sea, it really wasn't the same. Of course, once we had children, we'd need the extra rooms we had in the big house, but for now, a little getaway for just Cody and me sounded like the exact thing I needed to really feel at home.

I had slowed to a walk when my phone buzzed. I took it out of my pocket and answered. "Hey, Cody. What's up?"

"Finn called, and he found a few things he wants to ask us about. He wondered if we could head over to the newspaper to talk with him."

I looked behind me. "I'm about fifteen minutes from the house. I'll head back. I'll need to shower and dress, so you might let Finn know it will be awhile. If he needs someone to come by right away, you can go on ahead, and I can meet you there."

"Okay, I'll call him back and see what he thinks. I'll text you after I speak to him."

I slipped my phone back in my pocket, called to the dogs, and headed back in the direction from which

I'd come. I really hoped Finn could figure out who had been breaking into the newspaper. I was certain I wouldn't feel safe until this particular individual was behind bars.

Chapter 6

Finn was sitting at the reception desk waiting for Cody and me when we arrived at the newspaper. The men he had taking fingerprints and looking for physical evidence had all left by this point, so other than the crackle of Finn's radio, the place was quiet.

"You found something?" I asked as soon as we walked in the door.

Finn stood up. "I'm not sure. Maybe." He walked down the hallway, and Cody and I followed. Once he'd entered the morgue, he stood looking at the walls of shelves. Each shelf was divided into cubbyholes of sorts, and each cubbyhole held six months-worth of newspapers. Each section was labeled as January to June or July to December, followed by the year. "So each of these little sections of shelving holds twenty-six newspapers?" Finn asked.

"Approximately," Cody answered. "Orson did a special edition a few times, and depending on how the day of the week fell, there are a few sections with twenty-seven newspapers. Why do you ask?"

Finn walked over to the back wall. "All the shelving holding the older editions of the newspaper are pretty dusty. Didn't you have to remove the newspapers when you checked to see if any were missing?"

"No, we didn't need to remove them. We knew how many newspapers were supposed to be on each shelf and then just counted them, but I guess we should have taken the time to dust. It really does need to be seen to at some point."

"It may be a good thing that you hadn't actually dusted or removed the newspapers," Finn said. "He pointed to a section of the wall about halfway up on the right side. "The dust in front of the newspapers stored in these three sections of shelving has been disturbed. The dates listed on these shelving sections are January to June nineteen ninety-six, July to December nineteen ninety-six, and January to June nineteen ninety-seven."

"So you're thinking that whoever broke in was looking for something relating to an event that occurred between January of nineteen ninety-six and June of nineteen ninety-seven," I said.

"It's a theory, assuming, of course, that one of you hasn't removed the newspapers from these sections in the past few weeks."

"I haven't," I said. I looked at Cody. He shook his head.

"Is one of the newspapers missing?" Cody asked.

"I don't think so," Finn said. "I checked, and there are twenty-six in each section, so unless there was a special edition, they should all be here."

"So someone just wanted to look at the newspapers," I said.

"It seems that way," Finn confirmed.

"If someone wanted to look at one of the newspapers from this period, why didn't they just come to the front desk and ask to look at them?" Cody asked. "We do allow people to look at them as long as they do so here on the premises."

"I don't know," Finn admitted. "That would make more sense than breaking in to take a look, but to this point, all we have is the disturbed dust to go on. We haven't found anything else that would explain why someone would break in."

"So, what do we do now?" I asked.

"I guess we look at each and every page in each and every newspaper on those shelves and try to figure out what it was this person was after," Cody suggested.

I had a feeling we were in for a long night, but if going through all the newspapers with a fine-tooth comb would give us a clue as to why someone might have wanted to break in, I was up for it. I still wondered why the man or woman who'd broken in hadn't just asked to look at the newspapers, but perhaps they hadn't wanted anyone to know about whatever it was they were interested in. I also wondered why they didn't just take whichever newspaper they were after rather than putting everything back, but I supposed they had their reasons for doing that as well. For all we knew, they hadn't even been after the newspapers and moving them was just a coincidence or done to mislead us.

"How are we supposed to know which article this person was looking for, assuming someone had been looking for something specific?" I asked as I began my page-by-page inspection of the first newspaper in my stack.

"I have no idea," Finn said. "I guess we can eliminate ads as well as articles about bake sales, kiddie league games, and arts and crafts fairs. We should make notes if we come across anything really newsworthy such as a murder, suspicious auto accident, burglary spree, that sort of thing."

"The body of a man named Garwood Fielder was found on the side of the road along the old sawmill road on the north shore in August of nineteen ninety-six," Cody said. "The man had been shot, but as of the time this article was written, the person who'd shot him had still not been identified."

"That seems like the sort of thing we'll want to take a closer look at," Finn said. "Let's start a stack of editions to revisit. Once we go through everything, we can take a second look at the newspapers in that stack."

I was only seven years old in nineteen ninety-six, so chances are I wouldn't remember anything about any of the incidents we ended up finding. I wondered if it would be worthwhile to bring up the time frame to someone older who might remember if there had been anything significant going on. Perhaps my mother or Aunt Maggie, who'd both always been very involved in everything taking place on the island.

"I found an article relating to a series of house fires between January and April of nineteen ninety-seven," I said. "Fourteen structures were intentionally doused with gasoline and set aflame. The structures were empty at the time, so no one died, but a lot of people lost their homes. The arsonist, eventually identified as Roger Brown, was shot by his last victim, a man named Jason Willis."

"I'm not sure a case where the perpetrator was brought to justice would elicit action all these years later," Finn said, "but put it on the pile anyway."

"Here's an article from June of nineteen ninety-seven. A man was shot in the head while sleeping next to his wife in their bed," Cody said.

I wrinkled my nose. "I can't even imagine something like that happening. The poor woman. Does it say what happened, or who did the shooting?"

"This article just says that a woman named Margaret Reynolds called nine-one-one, claiming that a masked intruder broke into their home and shot her husband in the head while they slept. It was dark, the shooter wore dark clothes and a dark mask, and as soon as the deed was done, he left. She told the police that as far as she knew, her husband had no enemies, and she really couldn't imagine who would do such a thing."

"And they never caught the guy?" I asked.

Cody shrugged. "I really don't know. As of the time this article was written, the masked man had yet to be identified."

I looked at Finn. "Can you look it up? I don't know why I care about a crime that happened more than twenty years ago, but I find myself hoping the crime was solved so that the poor woman could move on and find some closure."

Finn set the newspaper he was looking through aside. "I guess it would just take me a minute or so to follow up. I doubt this case relates to whatever is going on now; however, if the crime was never solved, maybe someone has decided to pick up where law enforcement failed."

"So, do you think we're probably looking for an unsolved crime?"

"Maybe. The only reason I can come up with for anyone to sneak in here to look at an old newspaper is if someone decided all these years later to try to get justice for a crime that was never resolved."

"I suppose that could even explain why this individual didn't want to ask us for permission to look at a specific newspaper," Cody said. "If some guy is shot and killed two weeks from now and it's discovered that the victim of that shooting had, in fact, killed someone in the summer of nineteen ninety-seven, then anyone who'd come in to look at newspapers from the summer of nineteen ninety-seven would be an automatic suspect."

"Good point," Finn said. "I'll run next door and see what I can find out about our murder victim. What did you say his name was?"

Cody looked down at the newspaper. "John Reynolds."

"Okay. I'll go next door and look up the file. It'll probably be fifteen or twenty minutes."

"We'll be here," I promised Finn.

Cody and I continued to sort through the newspapers. Some we set aside to take a second look at, while others we stacked for reshelving. Neither of us had spoken for a good fifteen minutes when I came across something that seemed not only relevant but uber relevant as far as I was concerned.

"I think I may have something," I said.

Cody stopped what he was doing to give me his attention. "Oh. And what is that?"

"About six or seven newspapers back, I came across an article about the body of a woman fishermen found floating in the sea. Her left leg beneath her knee was missing, and it was suggested that perhaps she'd been the victim of a shark attack. I didn't think the article was relevant given what we're looking for, but now I've come across a commentary by Orson as to what he thinks might be going on."

"Going on?"

"According to this commentary, which is provided on page two in the same location as all the other commentaries Orson wrote, he had a source who was somehow able to lead him to evidence which allowed him to determine the identity of the woman found in the sea. Prior to this occurring, the woman had been labeled as a Jane Doe."

"Okay," Cody said. "Why is this relevant to what we're doing?"

"It's relevant," I said, "because prior to ending up in the sea, the victim, a twenty-one-year-old student named Lola Harvey, had been reported as missing by her college roommate. The woman was last reported being seen talking to a man with brown hair in a bar in downtown Seattle."

"That's quite a coincidence, but I doubt that missing person is related to our missing persons," Cody said. "That missing person went missing more than twenty years ago."

"I know," I said. "That was my first thought as well, but then I kept reading. It seems that Orson, who we know considered himself somewhat of an amateur sleuth, did some research and found out that other women had been reported as missing persons in the previous months. All were in their twenties, and all were the sort to frequent bars on the prowl for men. Five of the thirteen missing women had told a friend or loved one that they were heading to the islands for a romantic getaway with the man they'd just met."

"That does seem like quite the coincidence," Cody said.

"What's quite the coincidence?" Finn asked after rejoining us. He had a file in his hand, which drew my attention, but I decided to fill him in on the missing women and Orson's commentaries before asking about it.

"Did Orson say anything else?" Finn asked after I'd brought him up to speed.

"Not really. At least not in this commentary. I think we should look at the next couple of editions."

Finn sat down at the table and then slid the newspapers I'd had in front of me across the table so that they were in front of him. I wanted to protest since I had been the one to find the commentary in the first place, but he was the cop, and I was just the sidekick. I waited while he read.

"Orson did follow up," Finn said. "In the next edition, he mentions a witness who saw the woman who'd been found floating in the sea having a drink with an average-sized man with dark hair she referred to as Jack."

"There is no way this missing woman isn't connected to our missing women," I said.

"But why the long period of dormancy?" Cody asked. "If there is some guy out there named Jack who is picking up women in Seattle and then bringing them to the islands where he kills and disposes of them, why the gap?"

"Maybe there isn't a gap. Maybe he's been doing this the entire time," I suggested.

"I doubt it," Finn said. "The pattern would have been noticed long before this if women had been turning up missing every few months for more than twenty years. It seems more likely that something occurred that resulted in this killer going dormant. Maybe he's been in prison on another charge and just got out, or maybe he met someone, fell in love, and gave up his life of crime. Or maybe it was something else that made him stop only to start up again for an equally unknown reason."

Cody rested his arms on the table and leaned forward. "What else does it say?" he asked.

Finn looked down at the newspaper in front of him. "This commentary seems to suggest that Orson believed there was a serial killer at work, but he hadn't been able to convince law enforcement of that." Finn looked up. "I guess I can understand that. Orson had been able to identify the woman in the ocean as a missing person from Seattle, but at the time this commentary was written, it appears that's all he really had. Unless he had something that he hadn't yet published, it looks as if he hadn't come up with any sort of evidence to link this woman to the other twelve women who were missing from the Seattle area, and he certainly didn't have a basis to claim those women were dead. A lot of missing persons turn up much later, and many, it seems, have simply run away from a life that had become too overwhelming."

"Does Orson outline a plan to get the proof he needs?" I asked. "Orson would have done that. He was a man after the truth."

Finn nodded. "This article does promise his readers that he is hot on the trail of new evidence and will keep them updated as events unfold." He stopped reading. "I bet local law enforcement was not at all happy about that."

"Probably not," Cody said.

"Keep reading," I said.

Finn picked up the next newspaper and turned to page two. He raised a brow.

"What is it?" I asked. I should never have let Finn take the newspapers away from me.

"Orson keeps referring to a source he has yet to identify. In this edition, he tells his readers that his source was able to obtain copies of missing persons reports for thirteen women who had gone missing from Seattle between January of nineteen ninety-six and May of nineteen ninety-seven."

"How was he able to do that?" I asked.

"I don't know," Finn said, "but I doubt the reports were obtained legally."

"Maybe Orson's source was in law enforcement," I said.

"Maybe," Finn said, although his expression conveyed doubt.

"So go on," I encouraged. "Orson managed to get his hands on the missing persons reports for thirteen women who went missing over a seventeen-month period. Based on those reports, what conclusions did he come to?"

"He offers the reports as proof that a pattern existed," Finn said. "All the women were in their twenties, and all were reported as missing from Seattle or other towns along the Interstate 5 corridor.

Additionally, all were last seen on a Friday, and all had a reputation for hitting the bars on the weekends."

"Sounds like our current missing persons cases to me," I said.

Finn frowned. "Yes, I'm afraid it does."

"I guess this guy might be dumping all these women in the sea once he's done with them," Cody said.

"Possibly," Finn acknowledged. "There is really no way to know for certain at this point, but it would explain why none of the bodies of these missing women have turned up, assuming, of course, they're dead."

"What does the next newspaper say?" I asked.

Finn set the one he'd been looking at aside and opened the next one on the pile. He opened to page two. "Nothing. It's a guest commentary about zoning laws, which was written by Mayor Bradley."

I frowned. "And the one after that?"

Finn opened the next newspaper on the pile. "This commentary is about tourism and the effect of so many weekend visitors on the island."

"Someone shut him up," Cody said.

"But why?" I asked. "It sounds like he was really starting to get somewhere."

"I'm not sure," Finn said. "These commentaries have been printed in newspapers leading up to the beginning of tourist season. The idea of a serial killer on the island probably wouldn't have been good for tourism, so perhaps the mayor had a hand in ending the series."

That sounded like something Bradley would have done.

"Does anything in any of those commentaries help us figure out who is doing this now and how to stop them?" I asked. "Assuming, of course, that the same person was killing women back in the nineties and then again in current times."

Finn sighed loudly. "Not that I can see, but I'm going to go over everything again." He picked up the newspapers with commentaries relating to the missing women as well as the one about the woman found in the sea. "I know you don't usually allow these to leave the building, but I'm going to take them anyway. I'll be careful with them, and I'll bring them back when I'm done."

"Sure. No problem," Cody said.

"So, what did you find out about John Reynolds?" I asked. "Was his killer ever found?"

Finn shook his head. "Unfortunately, no. According to the report I managed to dig up, the house was searched extensively for any evidence linking a killer to the home. Nothing was found. Not a hair, not a fingerprint, not a single thing. Less than a month after her husband had been killed while sleeping next to her, Margaret Reynolds took her ten-year-old son and moved to the east coast. It appears that the sheriff filed the case away shortly after she left, and it's been collecting dust ever since."

"But why? Didn't he want to find the killer?"

"I'm sure he did, but you have to understand the man had nothing. What was he supposed to do?"

"There must have been blood spatter. A bullet to try to match to a gun."

"There was blood everywhere," Finn confirmed. "It was all over the bed, all over poor Mrs. Reynolds, all over the ceiling and the walls. The scene of the crime was a total bloodbath, but a gun was never found, there was no physical evidence, and like I said, the only witness was the wife who couldn't make out any details in the dark."

I slowly shook my head. "That poor woman. I really can't imagine."

"Other than the commentaries left by Orson, did you find anything else relevant to our current break-ins or the women who are currently missing?" Finn asked.

"Not really," Cody said. He slipped his hand over mine. He knew me well enough to know that I'd be upset by such a brutal murder. "It is possible, however, that Orson left notes behind that correspond with the commentaries. There may be notes to indicate what he eventually found out and why he stopped working on the case he seemed to be very involved with."

"Do you know where these notes might be?" Finn asked.

"At the house. Orson was a note taker, and he left boxes and boxes filled with notebooks, note pads, sticky notes, and even napkins with notes scribbled on them. I didn't want to throw them away, but they were taking up a lot of room down here, so I took them home and stacked them in an extra bedroom on the second floor we use for storage. I can take a look if you want," Cody offered. "There are a lot of boxes, and they aren't really organized, so it might take a while."

"Actually, looking for notes relating to these commentaries might be a good idea," Finn said. "Let me know if you come across anything."

Chapter 7

Cody and I picked up Italian food on our way home. He grabbed some wine while I grabbed the plates. I knew that Mr. Parsons valued having dinner with Cody and me when we were home for dinner, so we made a point of being home at least several times a week. Neither of us was really into cooking given our current schedules, so more often than not, we picked up take out and bought extra to leave in the refrigerator so that Mr. Parsons would have leftovers he could eat on the nights Cody and I ate out.

"So did you figure out who's been breaking into the newspaper?" Mr. Parsons asked after we'd settled in with our meals.

"We aren't certain, but it appears the break-ins might be related to a series of commentaries Orson wrote back in nineteen ninety-seven about women who'd gone missing from the Seattle area and he suspected had been brought to the islands to be killed and disposed of," Cody shared.

Mr. Parsons narrowed his gaze. "Now that you've mentioned it, I do seem to remember something about that. I should have thought of Orson's commentaries before, given the current situation with the missing women, but my mind isn't all that it once was."

"It appears Orson's theory was based on research he conducted after a woman was found floating in the sea," I added.

He nodded slowly. "I remember that. The woman looked to have been a shark attack victim. Part of her leg was missing. Orson, however, for reasons I don't quite remember, was certain the woman had been weighted and tossed from a boat. His theory was that when the shark attacked the weighted body, he freed her from the weight, which allowed the victim to float to the surface where she was found by fishermen passing by."

"I guess that makes sense," I said. "And if this guy is weighting his victims before dumping them into the sea, I guess that explains why the bodies of the other women were never found. Of course, there really isn't any way to prove that one way or another."

"That's true." Mr. Parsons stabbed at a meatball. "I remember Orson being quite determined to figure out what exactly was going on and to prove it." Mr. Parson chuckled. "I have to say that of all my friends, Orson was the orneriest. Once he latched onto a bone, he wasn't letting go for anyone."

"He said in the commentaries that he published that he had an informant he was working with," Cody said. "I don't suppose you know who that might have been?"

Mr. Parsons moved his head slowly from left to right. "No. I can't say as I ever did know."

"He also said he had been able to obtain copies of the missing persons reports for other women he felt fit the pattern," Cody continued. "Any idea how he got his hands on those?"

"No idea. As we both know, Orson was a sly one," Mr. Parsons said. "He had a way of getting whatever he needed to get to accomplish whatever it was he wanted to do. He was intelligent, persuasive, and, if need be, downright intimidating."

"Do you remember anything at all that he might have mentioned to you that he didn't publish in the newspaper?" I asked.

He paused to think about it. "I do remember that Orson rented a boat at one point. I seem to remember he had a couple of suspects in mind, although he hadn't settled on anyone. I remember that Orson got his hands on photos of the missing women and started looking for individuals who had seen them. He eventually determined that while most of the women had never been seen, a few of the missing women had been spotted in a variety of locations on several islands. It was Orson's theory that this killer made the rounds rather than bringing the women to the same location time and time again to avoid suspicion. He also seemed to think the killer had a home on one of the private islands where he could take these women and do whatever it was that he intended to do without being overheard or seen."

"There are a lot of private islands in the area," I said.

"Too many to check them out without knowing exactly what you're looking for," Mr. Parsons agreed.

"Thinking back, can you think of any reason Orson might have stopped writing the commentaries when he seemed so determined to follow his theory through to the end?" I asked.

Mr. Parsons took a sip of his water. "I don't remember him saying, but it seems to me that if there was a serial killer in the area and Orson was closing in on him, that might have put him in a dangerous situation. Orson had kids at home back then and a wife. People who he would have been motivated to protect. If the killer realized he was getting close and threatened his family, I could see him backing off even if he had, in fact, figured it out."

I understood that and I supposed if I was in that situation, I'd do the same thing.

After we finished our meal, Mr. Parsons settled into his little first-floor parlor with the two dogs and the cat. Apparently, the group had a movie planned for the evening. That was fine with me since Cody and I planned to go upstairs and begin going through the notebooks Orson had left behind. Just because Orson had never outed the killer in the newspaper, that didn't mean he hadn't left behind clues that might help us to identify him now.

"There are a lot of boxes up here," I said to Cody. "Any idea where to start?"

"Not a clue. As I pointed out to Finn, Orson left a lot of stuff behind. Notebooks full of notes, files. Even sticky notes with memos jotted down on them. There is a lot to go through."

I picked up a box, carried it to the center of the room, and opened the lid. I began sorting through it while Cody grabbed his own box.

"This box seems to have information relating to Orson's advertising clients," I said after a few minutes of looking through files.

"Grab a marker and label the box as advertising." He looked around the room. "Let's take the boxes we've already looked through into the room across the hallway. I'm afraid if we don't, we'll just keep looking through the same boxes over and over again."

"Good idea. We can bring them back in here and restack them when we're done."

Cody and I spent the next couple of hours sorting boxes. We'd decided not to take the time to really explore the boxes in any depth, but to simply set the boxes with notes and journals aside for further investigation and remove the boxes from the room which contained business files or customer contact information. Once we'd gone through all the boxes once, we began restacking those boxes we felt would be unlikely to have anything of use contained within them and taking the boxes with the most potential up to our living area, where we could go through them in comfort. The boxes we weren't sure what to do with were stacked along the far wall of the storage room. If we felt we needed to go through them again after having gone through those with the most potential, we'd be able to find them easily.

"I say we call it a day," Cody said. "It's late. The dogs need to go out. And we have all day tomorrow to look through the files in the boxes with the most potential. Besides, I'm beat."

"Yeah. Me too. I think we've done what we can for today, and I agree, tomorrow is soon enough to really dig into this." I walked over to the coat rack and grabbed my jacket. "Do you want to come with me? It's a beautiful night."

Cody smiled. "I do. Just let me grab my other shoes."

Once we were bundled up against the evening chill, we headed downstairs. Mr. Parsons was sitting in the kitchen, drinking a cup of hot milk. He informed us he was heading to bed when he was done but that he would leave his bedroom door cracked open for Rambler. Most nights, Rambler slept with Mr. Parsons, and Max slept with us, although they did hang out together for most of the day. I wasn't certain where Mystique would choose to sleep, although she seemed to have attached herself to Mr. Parsons. If she decided to go to bed with him, I'd just leave all the doors open in our living area so she could move about at will should she choose.

"It's a beautiful night," I said, as Cody and I set off down the beach, hand in hand, while the dogs ran on ahead of us.

"It really is. You can almost feel the promise of summer in the air." He tilted his head up toward the sky. "And those stars are really magnificent. They seem close enough to touch."

I bobbed my head slightly as I looked out toward the sea. I really missed sitting on the deck of my cabin, looking out at the moonlit sea, and wrapped in a heavy blanket against the chill brought about by the setting sun. "Do you remember that we discussed building a cottage or guesthouse on the beach when we made the decision to move in full-time with Mr. Parsons and give the cabin to Cassie?"

"I do," Cody said. "Are you still interested in something like that?"

"I am." I laid my head on his shoulder. "I've been thinking about how much I enjoyed sitting on the deck late at night or early in the morning and looking at the sea. I remember the peace I found listening to the waves at night as I laid in my bed under a mountain of blankets. I know a little cottage isn't practical for the long haul. I imagine we'll have children one day and need all those extra bedrooms in the big house. But maybe, for now, while it is still just the two of us, we could spend part of our time in a little bungalow of our own."

"I've already spoken to Mr. Parsons about it, and he is more than willing to allow us to build a guesthouse on the beach. He even offered to pay for it."

My eyes widened. "He did?"

Cody nodded. "Mr. Parsons considers us to be his family. He wants us to be happy, and he wants us to feel at home. He knows the move has been hard on you, and if a little cottage by the sea that we can use long term as a guesthouse will make you happy, he wants that for you. I was going to bring it up on several different occasions, but it's been so hectic since the move, and you hadn't mentioned it again, but if having our own space to escape to has been on your mind, I'll talk to some people and get some quotes."

I stopped walking and turned to hug Cody. "Thank you. We don't need anything big. A small structure like the cabin on Aunt Maggie's property would be perfect. Sometimes we can sleep there and at other times, we can sleep in the big house with Mr. Parsons. I do enjoy having coffee with Mr. Parsons in the mornings. He really is such a knowledgeable and interesting person."

Chapter 8

Friday, April 3

Our appointment at the bank did not go as we'd hoped, so once the loan manager had finished killing our hopes and dreams, Tara and I decided to head to her place for a cup of coffee and heart to heart conversation. When we arrived at her condo, I greeted her cat, Bandit, and then took a seat at the kitchen table while she made the coffee.

"I can't help but notice Danny's stuff strewn around the room," I said as casually as I could muster. "Is he living here now?" I'd wanted to ask that for weeks now, but somehow the timing hadn't been right. Actually, the timing wasn't right now either but delaying the more important and potentially emotional conversation we needed to have seemed like a good idea at the time.

"No, not officially," Tara said. She took the cream out of the refrigerator and set it on the counter. "He hasn't moved his stuff over, and we haven't actually had the 'living together' talk, but he has been sleeping here pretty much every night. I know the fact that we're trying again after so many failed attempts probably seems crazy to pretty much everyone in our lives, but we really do love each other, and I really do feel that we are meant to be together."

"Are you sure? I love you both, and I don't want to see you hurt again."

She poured coffee into the mugs and set them on the counter. "I don't want to get hurt again either, and I don't want Danny to be hurt again, but the time for playing it safe and protecting our hearts has come and gone. If we can't make it work this time, there is going to be pain. There is no avoiding that. But I feel that every relationship failure, every time we've broken up in the past, has taught us something both about ourselves and each other. I really think we're going to make it this time. I think Danny feels that way as well. I know you're worried about us, but what I really need is for you to be happy for us."

I smiled, placing my hand over Tara's. "If you're happy, I'm happy. And I will admit that Danny seems a lot more mature since he bought the bar with Aiden. I think having that level of responsibility has changed him."

"I think so too." Tara took a sip of her coffee. "So, what are we going to do about the bookstore?"

I hesitated, mostly because I had no idea what to say. The bank didn't seem to be willing to lend us the amount of money we'd determined we would need to supplement the payout the insurance company was offering. We really didn't want to tear down and rebuild the building, but after looking at the report provided by our insurer, simply repairing the place didn't seem like a viable option.

"Can I ask you something?" Tara asked when I didn't reply right away.

"Sure. Anything."

"How do you really feel about reopening the store?"

"What do you mean, how do I feel? It's what we want. Isn't it?"

"I didn't ask you what we wanted. I asked you what you wanted."

I have to say I wasn't expecting that question and had no idea how to reply.

"When we came up with the idea for Coffee Cat Books, it was a joint venture," Tara began. "You were mostly interested in the cat lounge as a way to find homes for your strays and deal with the overcrowding in the cat sanctuary, and I was mostly interested in owning a bookstore and running book clubs. The coffee bar was an afterthought that came about since we realized coffee would bring people into the store to look through our books and play with our cats. I guess at that point, the enterprise represented both our dreams, but things have changed to an extent. For one thing, the situation with the feral cats on the island is totally different than it was when Bradley was mayor. There aren't as many stays looking for homes, and over time, the cat sanctuary has become well known as the place to go for folks wanting to adopt whether they see them in the lounge or not. Not that the cat lounge wouldn't provide an option to really showcase those who are ready for forever homes, but since we've opened the store, your personal situation has changed."

"Changed how?"

"For one thing, you've reconnected with Cody and gotten married. Cody has purchased the newspaper, and since the store was destroyed and we were forced to close, you've been happily helping Cody investigate news articles. Since we first came up with the idea for Coffee Cat Books, you've also started helping Tansy with the magical cats that live on the island. In addition to everything else you have going on, that relationship seems to keep you pretty busy solving crimes."

"I guess that's true. I am busier than I was when we came up with the idea, and I have been happy working with Cody, but you are my best friend, and I am always happy when we're together. Owning and operating a bookstore was more your dream than mine, but I was happy working beside you every day. I want this for you. I know how much Coffee Cat Books means to you, and I want you to know that I'm not planning to bail on you."

Tara smiled. "I appreciate that. But I want you to be happy as well, and I'm not sure that spending forty to fifty hours a week at the bookstore is going to make you happy in the long run."

"So, what are you saying?" I asked. "Isn't the whole reason we're here is to come up with options now that the bank turned us down?"

She nodded. "Yes, that is partially why we are here. I've been thinking a lot about our options. The money we receive from the insurance settlement will probably allow us to open a store in another location. There are storefronts for rent in both Pelican Bay and

Harthaven with reasonable rents, but I just don't think it would be the same. Being right there on the wharf with the gorgeous view and proximity to the ferry was our greatest asset. I believe our location was the reason we were successful."

"I agree with that," I said.

"The bank suggested we might want to look into a private lender, or better yet, an investor who might give us the upfront money we need to rebuild in exchange for a small ownership share and the potential of investment income in the future."

"That seems like a good plan to me," I said. "I suppose we could ask around and see if anyone is willing to do that."

Tara leaned forward slightly. "Actually, I already have someone in mind. I wasn't sure I wanted to go that route until we had a chance to talk to the bank, but now that we have, I can see that an investor might be a good option. It would mean restructuring things. The investor would want a percentage of the business, and if we took on a partner, they would probably want to have some level of input into our decision making, which could get tricky if we didn't agree. Still, if an investor is the only option, I think it is one we should consider."

"I agree. Who are you talking about?" I asked.

"Balthazar Pottage."

I raised a brow. Balthazar Pottage certainly had more than enough money to buy a hundred businesses if he wanted, but he was an old man who had recently begun to turn things over to his son, Alex, once Tara and I had helped the father and son reconnect. I was surprised he was interested in taking on something new, although Alex did live with our part-time employee, Willow, and was helping her raise her son. I suspected there was more than friendship between the two, but as of this point, I didn't have any proof of that.

"You asked Balthazar to invest in Coffee Cat Books?" I asked.

"No. I didn't ask him. Willow called me last night, and we chatted for quite a while. We both know that she doesn't need the small paycheck she receives to get by since she's living with Alex, but she does enjoy the work, and it is important for her to have some money of her own. She's never been interested in working full-time, but the three days a week she does come in are really important to her. I guess she shared the details of our discussion with the insurance company with Alex, and he, in turn, shared our problem with Balthazar. Now that father and son are reunited, Balthazar wants Alex to be happy, and, of course, Alex wants Willow to be happy, and working at the bookstore seems to make Willow happy, so Balthazar called me with an offer. We still need to work out the details, and I realize that it wasn't all that long ago that I said I would never consider going into business with such a miser, but he is a totally different man now, and I really think it will be okay."

"Yeah," I said. "I think it will be okay. Balthazar is a totally different person now that Alex is back in his life. Actually, he's one of the people I thought about going to for a loan, but an investor we only needed to repay with a percentage of profit would be even better." I frowned. "I feel we've somehow gotten off topic. You asked me if I was happy at the bookstore. Are you thinking of going it alone this time?"

"Not if you still want to be part of things, but since we need to rework the ownership contracts and paperwork, now seemed like a good time to have this discussion with you. If you want to be an equal majority owner, then, of course, half is what you should have. Or at least half of our half once Balthazar takes his portion, whatever that works out to be. But if you are happier working with Cody, this would be a good time to open that door. Willow is still in for three days a week, and I've spoken to Cassie, and she's decided to split her time between the bookstore and the bar once the bookstore reopens. If you want to work full-time at the bookstore, then, of course, you are welcome to do so, but if you'd rather do something else..." She let the sentence dangle.

I took a moment to consider my options. I really did love working at the newspaper, and the bookstore had really only been a means to an end for me. "Are you planning to continue featuring the cats, whether I'm there or not?"

"Of course. The cats are part of who we are. Without the cats, we'd really just be a bookstore."

I had to admit I was tempted. I hadn't been a very good partner to Tara since I seemed to have one mystery after another to solve, which left her at the bookstore running things by herself most of the time. "I do love working with Cody, but I think I would miss everyone if I moved on from the bookstore entirely. Maybe I could do a part-time thing. Between Willow, Cassie, and myself, we'd make a full-time person, and if Cassie and I worked different days, we

83

could still bring the cats in every morning and then take them home at the end of the day."

Tara smiled a sort of sad smile that had me wondering if she was as okay with this as she said she was. "I think that would work perfectly. You, of course, would still own a share of the store, along with Balthazar and myself, since you were one of the original investors."

"How about we take my share and divide it between Cassie, Willow, and myself. You would own the majority share, which would give you ultimate control. I'm sure Balthazar would own the next largest piece, and Cassie, Willow, and I would all own a small piece, which would provide us with a sense of belonging."

"Are you sure?" Tara asked. "The last thing I want to do is to make you feel pushed out in any way."

"I'm sure. You were right when you said I was happy working with Cody. I think the option we've come up with will work out best for everyone. Two days a week at the bookstore and the rest of the time to chase down stories and solve mysteries sounds perfect to me, and, of course, if you ever need me to put in more time in the future, I'll be there for you. So, what do we need to do next?"

"I guess I should call Balthazar back and let him know that we are interested in looking at his offer. I'm assuming he'll be fair, but until we read his entire proposal, I guess we really can't know what he has in mind."

Chapter 9

Saturday, April 4

"Morning," I said to Mr. Parsons after filling a mug with coffee and sitting down at the kitchen table where he was working on his daily crossword puzzle.

"So, what are you and Cody up to today?" he asked after pushing the creamer in my direction.

"I guess we'll continue to sort through the boxes of items left behind by Orson. In a way, going through all that paper seems sort of pointless since we don't know what we're looking for, but Cody suspects that the person who has been breaking into the newspaper might have been looking for something other than a newspaper, so we're trying to cover all our bases."

Mr. Parsons bent over to pet Mystique, who'd wandered into the room from somewhere down the hallway. I hadn't noticed that she'd come upstairs last night, so she must have slept with Rambler and Mr. Parsons. Chances are she headed down the hallway to eat and use the cat box once she woke.

"I've been thinking about the discussion we had yesterday," he said. "I didn't think of it at the time, but it occurred to me at some point around two o'clock this morning that there was a man who regularly provided information to Orson. I don't know if he told him anything about the missing women, but he did tell him about all sorts of things. The man's name was Fairchild. I'm not sure if that was his first or last name. Fairchild is the only way Orson ever referred to him. I never met the man, but I know he lived on a boat which he kept docked in the private marina up on the north shore."

"Are you talking about the homeowner's marina up off Lighthouse Point?"

He nodded. "That's the one. Given the fact that the man lived on his boat, I don't think he owned a home there, but I suppose he might have had a friend with an open slip, or perhaps he rented one from someone. I know that Orson has been gone for a while now, and it's been even longer since he'd mentioned Fairchild to me, so I have no way of knowing if the guy is still around or if he's even alive. Still, it did occur to me that I should mention him to you."

"Do you think this man might have known something about the commentaries Orson wrote about the missing women?" I asked after refilling my mug.

"I don't know. I don't remember Orson specifically saying that he'd spoken to Fairchild about that particular story. What I do remember is that Orson would make comments about getting a tip from

Fairchild, and then he'd be off to follow up on it. He left me sitting alone in the bar a time or two when he got a call while we were out socializing."

"Okay, thanks. I'll mention it to Cody. I don't suppose it would hurt to follow up and see if the guy is still around. I don't suppose you know anything more about the guy. Maybe Orson mentioned what sort of work he did."

He shook his head. "No, I don't remember him mentioning anything like that. According to Orson, the guy seemed to come and go. I understand the boat he lived on was fully functioning, and sometimes he had it docked there at the marina while at other times he'd go off somewhere."

"I don't suppose you know how Fairchild came up with these tips he passed along to Orson?"

"No clue. Like I said, I never even met the guy."

"Okay, well, thanks. Any little tidbit of information is valuable at this point."

Once Cody came downstairs and joined us in the kitchen, he chatted with Mr. Parsons about Orson's informant while we ate. At some point, Cody decided it wouldn't be the worst idea to take a drive up north and see if we could obtain any additional information about Fairchild. It was unlikely he was still living on a boat docked in the same marina he'd been docked in all those years ago, but it was a beautiful day for a drive, and it never hurt to follow up on a clue. If nothing else, we figured we'd head over to the local bar and ask around.

We decided to take the dogs with us since there were a lot of deserted beaches along the way where we could let them out to run around. Not that the dogs weren't able to run around on our private beach most days, but they liked to go for rides, and I sensed they enjoyed the variety of having a different beach to explore from time to time. Mystique seemed to prefer to stay at home with Mr. Parsons, so after I checked her food, water, and cat box, Cody, the dogs, and I headed out.

It used to concern me when the cats who'd been sent to help me didn't start helping right away, but over the years, I'd learned that each cat had its own personality and its own rhythm. I'd also learned that if I simply waited until my feline friend was ready to help me, I could count on him or her to save the day when I needed them the most.

Twelve founding families from Ireland had settled on Madrona Island a very long time ago. Initially, the island had been divided up amongst those twelve families, but over the years, the land was sold and traded, and commercial areas evolved. The town of Harthaven was located on the west shore of the island. It was the oldest town on the island and the town where I grew up. The south end of the island was originally commercial in nature, but after the cannery closed and the ferry began bringing in visitors from Seattle and the surrounding area, the climate changed from warehouses to eclectic mom and pop shops. Coffee Cat Books is located on the wharf in Pelican Bay, the town that was established once people began moving to the area. It's a much more modern and progressive town than Harthaven and quickly became a haven for artists and touristy type shops.

The peninsula where Cody and I live with Mr. Parsons is divided into three large estates. The Hart Estate, currently owned by my older sister, Siobhan, and her husband, Finn, is in the center, while the estate owned by Mr. Parsons is to the south of that, and the estate owned by a woman named Francine Rivers is to the north. Mr. Parsons has informed Cody of his intention to leave his estate to Cody and me since he has no family. At first, that seemed like a lot to offer to someone you weren't related to by blood, but since returning to the island, Cody has taken care of him as if he was his own grandfather, and the land has to go to someone, so why not to the man Mr. Parsons loves like a grandson.

The north shore of the island, as well as the east shore, is sparsely populated. Those areas tend to attract rich landowners who enjoy their privacy, so it's on the north and east shore where you tend to find the larger gated estates, including the one owned by our good friend, Alex Turner.

There's a place known as the Hollow at the center of the island where the magical cats who live on the island make their home. The Hollow is a forested area that is surrounded by thick forest on every side. No human lives in the hollow, and few visit it, so the area is mostly left to the magical creatures that live there.

"So, what should we do first?" I asked as we neared the intersection where the roads that joined the east and north shore met.

"I guess let's head to the marina. Not that I expect this man to be there, but there might be someone around who knows him and might know where he can currently be found."

"And if no one is around?"

"Then we'll head over to that little bar that has the good fish and chips. We'll grab a bite to eat and ask around about Fairchild."

"And the dogs?" I asked.

"We'll bring them in. A place like that isn't going to mind."

When we arrived at the marina, we found it deserted, so we headed to the bar. As Cody predicted, neither the staff nor the other patrons seemed to care a bit that we had two dogs with us. We both ordered the fish and chips along with a pint of the beer on tap before Cody asked the man who took our order about the man we were there to find.

"Yeah, I know Fairchild," the man said. "Lived here in the marina for decades until the man who owned the slip he rented up and sold his home and the slip along with it. Fairchild couldn't find anyone else here in this marina to rent to him, so he moved his boat over to Lopez Island."

"There are a lot of slips for rent in Pelican Bay," I pointed out.

"Too crowded. Harthaven is too. Fairchild values his privacy. He has a nice thing on Lopez Island. He's tied up at a private dock owned by some tech magnate who has a mansion on the island, but is rarely there."

"Do you know how we can get ahold of him?" Cody asked.

"He doesn't have a phone. If you want to find out exactly where he's docked, ask at the marina. They should be able to give you directions."

"Thanks. I'll do that."

As predicted, the fish and chips were delicious. After we ate, we took the dogs for a run on the beach and then headed back south. When we got home, Mr. Parsons greeted us, and we filled him in. It was much too late to head over to Lopez Island today, but maybe we could go tomorrow. I asked Mr. Parsons about Mystique when I didn't see her anywhere in the area, and he told me the cat had headed upstairs over an hour ago, and he hadn't seen her since. I was sure the cat was fine, but I decided to check on her while Cody and Mr. Parsons tried to figure out what we should make for dinner.

"What did you do?" I asked the cat, who was sitting atop one of the many file folders scattered across the floor of our living room. It appeared as if she'd dumped several of the boxes we still needed to go through onto the floor and then scattered everything around.

"Meow," she said with a look of complete innocence.

I bent over and began picking up files until it eventually dawned on me that perhaps there was something special about the file Mystique was sitting on. I shooed her aside, picked up the file, and opened it. I read the first page of the small stack of documents contained within. I looked down at the cat. "I think you might be onto something."

Chapter 10

One of the things contained in the file was a list of names. Based on the handwriting, the list appeared to have been penned by Orson. All thirteen of the names on the list were female names, and next to each name was a date. The first date was January twenty-fourth of nineteen ninety-six. The next one was March eighteenth of the same year, and the last one was May twenty-ninth of nineteen ninety-seven. Copies of missing persons reports matching the names of all thirteen women on the list were beneath the list. All the reports were associated with women in their twenties who were reported missing from several different towns along Interstate 5 from Tacoma to Bellingham. The current missing women Finn had been investigating had all lived in Seattle and had all been last seen in Seattle, but if Orson was onto something during the first missing persons spree, then perhaps Finn should widen his search for other women who seemed to fit the pattern.

I grabbed the file and took it downstairs, where Cody was chatting with Mr. Parsons. "Look what Mystique found." I laid the folder on the table.

Cody picked it up and looked inside. "Missing persons reports?"

"They correspond to the missing women Orson seemed to be writing about in the nineties. I haven't had a chance to take more than a quick glance at the reports, and I'm not sure if the information contained within can help us, but Mystique seemed to want me to look inside the file, so I think we should take a close look at everything."

Cody pulled a piece of lined paper from the bottom of the stack. "It looks like in addition to the copies of the missing persons reports, Orson left notes."

"So, what do they say?" Mr. Parsons asked.

Cody frowned. "A lot of this is in some sort of shorthand and really doesn't make any sense to me. The initials JPR come up fairly often as do the initials MR and DF." Cody glanced at Mr. Parsons. "Do any of those initials mean anything to you?"

"No. Not off hand. I suppose if we take the content surrounding the initials into account, we might be able to make some sense of what he noted."

"There are a few times and dates, but otherwise, there are disjointed words that when read linearly make no sense," Cody shared. "Like I said before, it appears Orson used some form of shorthand to make his notes. The fact that the words make no sense might very well be intentional so that no one except for him can read what he wrote."

I picked up the pile of papers that Cody had set back down on the table. Mystique had gone to a lot of trouble to make sure I'd see this particular file, so there must be something contained within that I needed to see. I supposed the thing she wanted me to see might simply be the missing persons reports. The reports demonstrated that there had been missing women in the nineties all up and down the coast, so maybe that was the piece of information she wanted me to share with Finn. But my gut told me there was something more. A clue of sorts that might be hiding within the notes Orson had left. A clue, I suspected, that was waiting to be decoded and understood.

"I think I'm going to go over it again later," I said. "I just have this feeling there is something more to discover that we haven't noticed yet." I glanced at Mr. Parsons. "I was thinking about grilling tonight. Do you feel like sitting out on the patio?"

"Actually, that sounds lovely. I really haven't been out much at all since the cold weather set in, but based on today's weather report, it looks like we might be in for a warming trend."

"It's actually supposed to rain next week, but once the rain is gone, it should be sunny and warm for the next couple of weeks. When Cody and I were walking the dogs on the beach earlier, it was almost too warm for the long sleeve t-shirts we had on." I glanced at Cody. "Why don't you start a fire in the pit while I make the salad. That way, if it does cool down, we can warm up next to it."

"Will do," Cody said, heading out the back door to the patio.

I'm not sure why Mr. Parsons' grandfather put the patio area at the back of the house when he built the house since the ocean and the superior view was in the front. The patio area was nice and cozy, but I always had thought that not taking advantage of the exceptional view was sort of a waste.

"I spoke to Cody earlier," Mr. Parsons said as I began chopping lettuce for a salad. "He mentioned that you might want to go ahead with the plans we discussed and build a little cottage out near the water."

I paused. "Is that okay? This is your home, and I wouldn't want to do anything you weren't comfortable with."

"It's more than okay. In fact, I think it's a wonderful idea. A cottage will provide a little hideaway for you and Cody right here on the property, and maybe at some point in the future after you have children and need the room the larger house will provide, you can use it as a guesthouse."

"That's exactly what Cody suggested. I do love living here with you, but if I am totally honest, I miss the intimacy of my own space."

"I understand completely. Cody is going to have some plans drawn up, and we'll take it from there."

I crossed the room and hugged the man I'd always been fond of but had grown to love since living in his home. "Thank you. This really means a lot to me."

"I know it isn't the dream of every new bride to move in with the old man who lives next door, and I appreciate that you and Cody look out for me the way you do. To tell you the truth, I'm happy to have a chance to do something to repay your kindness."

Chapter 11

Sunday, April 5

"I think seven down is algae," I said to Mr. Parsons the following morning while having coffee with him before heading to church and then visiting Lopez Island.

"I think you might be right," he smiled.

"Cody and I are going to be gone for most of the day, but Cody spoke to Banjo and Summer, and they assured him that they will be by later for lunch and a movie." Banjo and Summer were a hippie couple who lived in a little shack down the beach. The distance by road between their property and Mr. Parsons' was actually quite far, but the walk down the beach between the two residences could be accomplished within a few minutes.

"I don't need a babysitter," he reminded me, "but I am happy to visit with my friends. It'd already been

97

a couple weeks since they'd been by when I came down with that darn flu. I'm feeling much better now, however."

"I know they missed you as much as you missed them, and Cody wanted to be sure you had someone to help you with the dogs since your leg has been bothering you. I went to the store on Thursday, so there's plenty of food to make whatever you're in the mood for."

"Thank you, dear. You and Cody have a nice day. And don't forget to take the file to pass along to Finn. I think he might be interested in the story Orson was working on."

"I agree. I think he will be very interested indeed."

Cody and I both attended Saint Patrick's Catholic Church, where we oversaw the youth choir. When I was first asked to take over the choir, I wasn't sure I wanted to do it, but since making the decision to take on the responsibility, I'd grown very fond of all the children we worked with every week. This morning, Cody offered to head to the choir room to get the group ready while I went in search of Finn. I wanted to hand over the file I'd found before mass in the event he, Siobhan, and Connor left before I connected with them once mass was over. I'd made copies of each and every page I planned to pass off to Finn since somewhere in the back of my mind, a little voice was telling me I was going to need the information contained within it at some point in the future.

"Oh good, you're here," I said to Finn after having bent down to hug Connor. "I have the file I told you about when I called last night."

He opened it and peeked inside. "Okay, thanks. I'll take a look and see what I can make out of it. Are you and Cody still heading to Lopez Island today?"

I nodded. "As soon as mass is over. I'm not sure we'll even be able to track down this Fairchild, and even if we can, I'm not sure he knows anything about the missing women, but we figured it was worth a try."

"I agree. Call me when you get back. Call me sooner if you need anything.'

"I will." I looked toward the hallway leading to the choir room. "I should head to the choir room to help Cody. I'll talk to you later."

"Has Mom cornered you yet about Easter next week?" Siobhan asked before I could make my escape.

"No. Is she planning something?"

"She wants the whole family to get together. I don't think Aiden will be back from his fishing trip by then, but I told her that Finn, Connor, and I would be willing to host at our place."

"We should be able to come," I said. "I'll need to check with Cody, and we should invite Mr. Parsons."

"Everyone is invited. Mom was going to call Aunt Maggie and invite her and Michael, and I'm sure Danny will invite Tara. I think Mom was going to mention it to Marley and Sister Mary as well."

"Sounds like fun. I'll talk to Cody, but you should go ahead and count us in."

By the time I got to the choir room, Cody had everyone ready to make the procession into the church. He took the front of the line while I fell into the back to keep an eye on things. Most of the kids who signed up for choir were fairly well behaved, but it seemed that we had a couple of pranksters every year who we really needed to keep an eye on.

Once mass was over, I mentioned the Easter event to Cody, then after confirming with Siobhan that Cody and I would attend the Easter gathering, we headed toward the ferry terminal. There wasn't time to waste if we were going to make the next ferry heading to Lopez Island, so we went straight there and got into line.

"The ferry should be here in about ten minutes," Cody said.

"I wish we would have had time to eat after church. All I had this morning was coffee."

"We can eat once we get to Lopez Island. They have that cute restaurant you like with the fish sandwich."

"That does sound good. I hope this trip doesn't turn out to be for nothing. It's such a nice day, it feels wrong not to be lounging around on the beach."

"The spring weather is just getting started. There will be plenty of sunny days to enjoy. By the way, speaking of sunny days, I spoke to Mr. Parsons, and he's fine with us building a cottage close to the water."

"He told me. He really has gone out of his way to make us comfortable since we moved in full-time."

"He wants us to be happy. I spoke to a friend of mine who works in construction, and he said that if we are looking to build something small and are willing to start right away, he might be able to fit it in before he's due to start work on the office building that's going in west of Pelican Bay later this summer."

"I'm game to do it right away if you are," I said to Cody. "I know exactly where I want to put it. There's that flat spot close the water yet off to the side. I think I'm going to have just a single story so it won't interfere with the view from any of the windows in the big house. We'll need to put a walkway between the drive and the cottage, but that should be easy. I'm thinking one bedroom, a bathroom, a small living area, a small kitchen, and a large deck for entertaining."

"That sounds perfect. I'll have it drawn up this week, and maybe we can start the week after Easter."

The ferry docked, and the line of cars began to drive forward. We were shown which level to park on and then asked to turn off our engine for the ride over to the island. Once everyone was aboard, the ferry pulled away from the dock. It was a short ride, but it was such a nice day that Cody and I decided to go up to the passenger deck so we could enjoy the water and the sunshine.

Once Lopez Island came into sight, we headed back down to the car deck, where we would follow the line of cars onto the island after we docked.

The restaurant Cody and I had decided on was right on the water. It was Sunday, and therefore busy, but we still managed to find a table on the outdoor deck. I ordered my favorite fish sandwich, and Cody ordered roast beef and macaroni salad. I hadn't worn sunscreen, nor had I worn a hat, so I hoped the sun would move on around so a nearby tree would shade us before too much more time went by.

"So, what exactly is the plan?" I asked Cody after we'd ordered.

"I guess we'll ask around and see if anyone knows Fairchild or where we can find him. If we can get a location, we'll head over to where his boat is docked and see if he'll speak to us. There's a chance he's not around, and there is an equal chance that even if we find him, he won't speak to us, but we both decided it was worth the time it took to make the trip to find out."

"I agree. It is."

The waiter set my plate in front of me. The roll was baked on-site, and the tartar sauce was homemade. The breaded fish fillet was usually made from the catch of the day, so it was fresh as well.

"This is delicious," I said after taking my first bite.

"This roast beef is excellent as well. I think it's the fresh rolls that really make the difference." He took a sip of his wine. "By the way, I've been meaning to talk to you about something."

"Uh, oh. That doesn't sound good."

"It's not bad. Exactly. More like unexpected."

I felt the knot in my gut I'd been struggling with beginning to tighten. "Unexpected?"

"My mom called yesterday. She wanted to let me know that she's planning to visit us this summer."

I really tried to force a smile. "I see. That's great — really — really — great."

"I know my mom can be a challenge, but she is my mother," Cody reminded me. I suspected he was expecting an argument from me, but I'd already decided a long time ago that no matter how crazy Mrs. West made me, she was my mother-in-law, and I would love her to the best of my ability.

"Yes. I am aware that she's your mother. It's right there on your birth certificate and everything."

"And she hasn't been to Madrona Island since the wedding. I know we've been to Florida a couple of times since then, but she did point out that she hasn't been here."

"It has been a while," I agreed. "Did she happen to say when she might come?"

"She mentioned July."

"July is a lovely month here on the island. Did she mention how long she might stay?" *Please, please say she only has time for a short visit.*

"A month. Maybe up to five or six weeks."

I really tried not to groan, but I'm pretty sure I heard a tiny groan slip out.

"That's wonderful." I smiled so hard my face felt like it might shatter. "Really, really, wonderful." I took a gulp of wine. "I suppose we might want to see if that hotel she stayed in the last time has any rooms. She did seem to enjoy her stay there, but they fill up fast."

"Actually," Cody said, visibly pulling away, "she thought that since we've moved into that nice big house with all the extra bedrooms, she might just stay with us."

I grabbed the wine bottle and topped off my glass. I drank it down in one long swallow. "With us." I took a deep breath. "That's really — wow — that really is unexpected." I glanced at Cody, who was looking at me with an apology written all over his face. I knew he wasn't any happier about this than I was, so once again, I forced a smile. "But great," I added. "Just so great."

He put a hand over mine. "I'm sorry. I tried to talk to her about a hotel, but she seemed adamant. I suppose I could tell her that Mr. Parsons is uncomfortable with that, but we both know he won't mind a bit. In fact, I suspect that he and mom will get along just fine."

Actually, I suspected Cody was right about that. "It's fine. Really. She is your mother, and she has every right to visit her son any time she wants. If I feel like I need a break, I'll just stay with Cassie for a couple of days."

He tucked a lock of hair behind my ear. "Thanks for not freaking out. I know having her here is going to be challenging, but I think together we can get through it."

"We will," I agreed, knowing even as I said it that five to six weeks in close proximity to the woman who seemed to want to change everything about me was probably going to land me in the loony bin.

After we ate, we headed toward the closest marina, hoping to find someone who knew where we might find Fairchild. As it turned out, Fairchild wasn't all that hard to find. As we'd been told yesterday, his boat was docked at a huge estate that served as a vacation home for a tech millionaire who lived in Seattle.

"Permission to come aboard?" Cody called out after we arrived at the boat.

A man with a scraggly gray beard and equally gray hair poked his head out from the cabin below. "And who might you be?" he asked.

"My name is Cody West, and this is my wife, Cait. Orson Cobalter was a friend. In fact, I bought the *Madrona Island News* from him when he decided to retire."

"Retire? The guy is dead."

"Yes, I know Orson is dead," Cody said. "But he retired before he died, and that's when I decided to buy the newspaper. Anyway, the reason I'm here is because I hoped to speak to you about some information you provided to Orson back in the nineties."

"I provided a lot of information to Orson over the years. What information are you specifically asking about?"

"The women who went missing between nineteen ninety-six and nineteen ninety-seven."

"Ah." The man walked more fully onto the deck. "I heard there have been some new cases that seem eerily similar."

"So, do you know anything about these women?" Cody asked.

The man spit into the water. "I know something about everything."

Cody looked at me. I shrugged.

"We were hoping to pick your brain in regards to these missing women if you're willing," Cody said.

"You have cash?"

"Cash?" Cody asked.

"I'm an informant, not a freaking charity. If you want to know what I know, you're going to need cash."

"How much?" Cody asked, pulling his wallet out.

"A hundred bucks will get you invited aboard. We'll have some whiskey and talk a bit. Depending on how that goes, we can work things out from there."

Cody pulled five twenties out of his wallet and handed them to the man.

"Okay. Come on aboard. I'll grab the whiskey and some glasses, and you can ask me your questions."

I had to admit that the man was an interesting sort.

"So, what do you want to know?" the man asked after throwing back what I suspected would be the first shot of many.

"Back in nineteen ninety-six, a woman was found floating in the sea by some fishermen," Cody began. "Her leg had been severed beneath the knee, and most everyone figured she was the victim of a shark attack and left it at that. The woman didn't have an ID on her, of course, and her body had been pretty mutilated after being in the sea, so she was listed as a Jane Doe. There was an attempt to figure out who the woman actually was, but after a bit of a search, nothing popped, so law enforcement personnel in the area moved on to other things. Orson, however, was like a dog with a bone. He became really invested in figuring out who this Jane Doe actually was, so he began to dig deeper. At some point, he came across what he was sure was a pattern involving women missing from bars along the Interstate 5 corridor. It took him a while to put everything together, but he eventually settled on a theory that these women were being taken from bars by a man with brown hair and then brought to the islands where they were killed and disposed of. He tried to get Tripp on board," he referred to the resident deputy at the time, "but Orson didn't have proof that the women had even been on the islands, and he certainly didn't have a single stick of evidence that they had been killed here and then dumped in the sea. He was able to eventually find a missing woman from amongst those he scraped together from several law enforcement jurisdictions who he was certain was Jane Doe. It took him a while, but eventually, they were able to prove this as being so."

"Sounds like you already know quite a bit," Fairchild said.

"We have initiated our own investigation. I guess what I'd like to know at this point is where you fit into this whole scenario. How exactly did you help Orson, and what might you know that we haven't stumbled across yet?"

Fairchild cleared his throat, then spit onto the floor next to him. I wanted to vomit but somehow managed to hold onto my lunch. Eventually, he began to speak. "After Orson matched the Jane Doe who'd been found with one of the missing women, he became determined to figure out what had happened to the other missing women that fit the profile he'd come up with, so he asked me to help. I get around. I know a lot of people, and I hear things. Plus, I'm not a cop, so people who won't talk to cops will talk to me. Orson and I had been working together for a while, and we had a payment system in place, so when he asked for my help, I took the photos of the missing women he provided me and began scouring all the bars on all the islands, looking for someone who had seen any of the missing women."

"And did you find anything?" I asked.

"Not at first, but after a bit of time, I was able to find a single bartender on San Juan Island who admitted to me that he had seen one of the women. He told me that the woman came in with a man with dark hair who she referred to as Jack. He also said she was obviously on something since she was totally out of it the entire time they were together in the bar. The bartender swore he had never seen either the girl or the guy before, nor had he seen them since. Of course, even though this tip told us very little, it was something, and Orson became even more resolved to find the others. It took us at least a month, but we eventually found witnesses who indicated that three of the women Orson was looking for had 'probably' been on one of the islands with a man with brown hair at some point."

"Do you remember which islands?" I asked.

"San Juan and Orcas, but keep in mind these are unconfirmed sightings. For all we know, none of the women had actually been seen on any of the islands. Orson and I discussed the fact that if this man named Jack had kidnapped these women with the intent of killing them, it was unlikely he would take them to a public bar."

I supposed Fairchild had a point. It did seem unlikely the women the bartenders identified were actually the same women Jack had kidnapped and killed, assuming, of course, the kidnapper's name was even Jack, which we certainly didn't know for a fact at this point.

"Did Orson ever come up with anything else?" Cody asked. "Did any of the other bartenders on any of the other islands recognize Jack?"

"Not really. In fact, I'm pretty sure that it was Orson's belief that the women the bartenders had identified weren't actually the women he was looking for. Still, he did suspect the women had been brought to the islands. Orson was able to track down friends and family members of the missing women he'd identified, and was eventually able to find three people who shared with him that before they'd gone missing, the woman in question had either called or texted them to let them know they were going to the islands for a romantic getaway with some guy they'd just met."

"At this point, was he getting the local law enforcement team to take his theory seriously?" I asked.

"Yes and no. Tripp seemed to give Orson the attention he felt his theory deserved, but he really didn't know how to help. Even though Orson had found three bartenders to say that they thought they recognized one of the women in the missing persons photos, I don't think any of them were really all that certain of who they'd seen. I kind of felt bad for the guy. He met with obstacle after obstacle, but he wasn't giving up even though he really hadn't come up with anything concrete."

"But he did give up," I pointed out. "He seemed to be hot on the trail of this man he was certain was a serial killer and then poof, the commentaries came to an end as abruptly as they began. Do you have any idea why?"

"Honestly, I'm not sure. There was a point near the end of May in nineteen ninety-seven, when he seemed to have figured something out. He never did tell me what he'd figured out, but I could see the gleam in his eyes that he always got when he'd managed to solve a mystery. I was really expecting him to come out with the big reveal in that newspaper of his, then the next thing I knew, he was dropping the whole thing. I asked him why he was dropping his investigation when it seemed like he was so close, but he never really explained. My suspicion at that time was that this Jack guy found out what Orson was doing and threatened someone Orson loved. I can't imagine any other reason he'd simply walk away from the whole thing. The interesting thing is that after Orson stopped looking for the guy, women stopped going missing. At least women who fit the pattern Orson had established. I sometimes wonder if Orson didn't cut some sort of a deal with the guy. Guess with Orson dead, we'll never know what really happened."

"It looks like there is a whole new set of missing women fitting the same MO. Any idea why this guy might have started up again?" Cody asked.

Fairchild shrugged. "I guess if Orson and this Jack did have a deal that prevented Jack from continuing to do whatever it was he was doing, he might have found out that Orson was dead and decided the deal he cut had died along with the man."

"Do you know anything else that might help us to figure out both what went on back then, and what is going on now?" Cody asked.

Fairchild downed a shot. "Perhaps."

"Would you mind sharing what you know?"

"For another hundred bucks."

Cody opened his wallet. "All I have left is forty."

He reached out his hand. "Forty will get you a clue or two." He put the two bills in his pocket. "Back when the women were going missing in the nineties, Tripp, as well as pretty much all the other law enforcement officers, were certain this man who they suspected had been picking these women up and bringing them to the islands, lived in Seattle, but had a vacation home on one of the islands. Orson told me that he thought it was the other way around. He thought the guy lived here on one of the San Juan Islands but used Seattle and the other towns he'd identified as a hunting ground. It was his opinion that this man was probably someone known to others living on the same island as he did. Orson felt certain he lived a somewhat normal life with the exception of his little hobby, and that during those times he wasn't picking up women and killing them, he probably seemed like a totally normal guy."

"Well, that's frightening," I said.

"Did Orson have a theory as to which island this guy might have lived on?" Cody asked.

"Actually, he was fairly certain the man he was looking for lived on Madrona Island."

Chapter 12

Monday, April 6

As had been predicted, a storm blew in overnight, which meant my long run on the beach would have to wait. Cody had meetings set up with advertisers, which was not an activity I was interested in, so after I had breakfast with Mr. Parsons, I took the dogs out for a quick run, and then I headed upstairs to continue working on the boxes Cody had stored in the house. The idea that this man named Jack, who theoretically had kidnapped and killed a bunch of women back in the nineties and might very well be back at it again, actually lived on Madrona Island, had me spooked a lot more than I was willing to admit. Of course, Fairchild didn't seem certain of this fact, and so far, I hadn't found anything in Orson's notes to indicate as much, but the more I thought about it, the more the concept seemed to make sense. When I'd believed this serial killer lived and worked in Seattle, which is where he seemed to hunt for his victims, the threat felt removed from those I loved and cared about. But if this madman did live on the island, if he lived and worked here amongst us, that left me with a different feeling altogether. Sure, it did seem that he picked his women up elsewhere and then brought them back to the islands to die, which I supposed was somewhat of a comfort, although I had no idea why. Any way you diced it, the whole situation really was horrific. Still, having this man living close by gave me extra chills. My brothers owned a bar, and both my sister and my best friend worked at that bar. Were they in danger if this madman really was killing women once again?

I sat down on the floor in the living room where I had a warm fire and large picture windows facing the sea. I set the first box on the floor next to my feet. I opened the lid, took out a stack of notebooks and files, and set them on the floor next to one of the floor to ceiling windows. I'd barely begun to sort through the box when Mystique trotted into the room and crawled into my lap.

"Have you finally decided to help me?" I asked.

"Meow." She laid down on top of the notebook I'd begun to look through and began to purr.

"I'm afraid we have work to do. Break time can come later. I don't suppose you want to point me in a direction as long as I'm stuck here in the house looking through these boxes."

"Meow." She got up and headed toward the wall where we'd stacked the boxes.

"You want me to get a different box?"

"Meow."

"Okay, which one? There are dozens of boxes in here."

Mystique trotted over to one of the stacks and began pawing at a box that was stacked third from the bottom. I set the boxes on top of it aside and opened the lid. "More notebooks and files. Do you want me to look through this one?"

"Meow." With that, she turned and headed back toward the rug where we'd been sitting.

I picked up the box and followed her. I set the box down and opened the first file to find a copy of the police report relating to the man who'd been shot in the head while sleeping next to his wife.

"This file isn't related to the missing women. Do you want me to look into this unsolved murder instead?"

"Meow." Mystique laid down on the floor near me and began to purr.

"You realize it might not be a good idea to get distracted with a different case. I know we haven't made a lot of progress on the missing persons cases, but we are making some headway, and due to the link with the current missing women, it seems a bit more timely."

Mystique got up and laid down on the file in front of me. She began to purr.

"Okay. If you're sure. Scooch on over and I'll take a look to see if I can figure out what it is you're trying to show me."

The cat moved over, and I opened the file. As we'd already learned from the news articles Orson had written, a man named John Reynolds was shot in the head and killed while he slept next to his wife, Margaret Reynolds. Margaret told the police that she hadn't heard a thing until she heard the gunshot, which woke her. She saw a man in black clothes and wearing a black mask fleeing. When she realized her husband had been shot, she called nine-one-one. Her husband was probably dead before Mrs. Reynolds even woke up enough to realize what was happening. The local deputy investigated the murder of Mr. Reynolds, but he never found one bit of evidence to suggest who might have been responsible for such a gruesome crime. There was no sign of forced entry, although Mrs. Reynolds did say that they rarely bothered to lock their doors. A crime scene team was brought in to dust for prints and look for physical evidence that might have been left behind, but not a single trace of evidence was found.

Shortly after Mr. Reynolds was murdered, Mrs. Reynolds moved back east with her son, Alton, who was just ten at the time. Alton had been spending the night at the home of one of his friends from school when his father was shot, so he hadn't seen or heard anything and had been unable to aid in the investigation in any way.

"So, what am I looking for?" I asked the cat. "This is all the same information provided to us by Finn the other day."

The cat swatted at the page. It seemed she wanted me to turn the document over, so I did. Notes penned in Orson's handwriting were on the back. Most of it looked like gibberish, but I did notice the initials JPR, which had been circled in red. Hadn't JPR been one of the initials I'd found in the box with notes relating to the missing women? I got up and opened that box to confirm that indeed the same initials had been jotted down on the lined paper included with the missing persons reports that Orson had somehow obtained.

"Are you saying these cases are linked in some way?" I asked the cat. "I really don't see how. I mean, I suppose it's possible that the same man we suspect was kidnapping and killing young women he picked up in bars might have killed this man, but why?"

"Meow."

"And what does JPR stand for? John Reynolds? I suppose the P could be associated with his middle name." I picked up my phone. "I suppose Finn would know."

I called Finn and confirmed that John Reynolds legally had a hyphenated last name, which made his full legal name John Peyton-Reynolds. I supposed that meant that Orson had been trying to link the two cases in some way, but why? Maybe John had found out who it was that had been kidnapping and killing the young women which created a situation where this brown-haired man known as Jack might have felt it necessary to kill him to keep him quiet. Could Jack have been a neighbor? Coworker? Friend? I really wasn't sure how we could find out at this point.

After hanging up with Finn, I got up and crossed the room to look out the window. The sea was angry, and the waves large, as gale-force winds pushed them onto the shoreline. Rain pelted the window, making quite the racket as the sky opened up. I loved the sunny skies we'd been enjoying, but there were times when a stormy day matched my mood much better than a blue sky and calm sea.

I thought about what we knew or at least suspected we knew about Jack. The truth of the matter was that we really didn't know anything.

Orson had left notes indicating that someone named Jack had brought one of the missing women to a local bar, but after speaking with Fairchild, even that seemed to be an unconfirmed piece of information. We also knew that there was a cocktail waitress who worked for the Yellow Feather on San Juan Island, who claimed that a man named Jack had been in the bar bragging about bringing women to the island for a unique sexual experience. This didn't mean he killed them, and it was quite possible the women came willing and left happily at the end of their stay.

Both the Jack from the nineties and the Jack associated with the women who were currently missing had been described as having brown hair. I wondered about the lapse in time. If Jack with brown hair from the Yellow Feather had been the same man who'd kidnapped and killed women in the nineties, wouldn't his hair be gray by now? Of course, lots of men died their hair, and some men grayed very late in life. I supposed it might be worthwhile to ask Cody and Finn if either of them had asked the witnesses they'd interviewed what the approximate age of their Jack might be.

The rain let up just a bit as I stood there watching it. Mystique wandered over, so I picked her up and hugged her to my chest. She certainly was a soft and fluffy cat. She seemed to like human contact, and I knew Mr. Parsons adored her. I wondered if she might stay around once her job was done. The other cats I'd had all moved on once they had helped me do what we were destined to do, but Mystique had bonded with Mr. Parsons to the extent that I wouldn't be at all surprised if she decided to stay.

"So, what do you think?" I asked the cat. "Do I continue to look through the box associated with the shooting or return to the box with the information relating to the missing women Orson identified?"

"Meow."

I set her on the floor, and she wandered into the kitchen and began pawing at the pantry door.

"Are you hungry?"

"Meow."

"The cat food is in the laundry room. Remember, I showed you where you could find both your food and water."

She continued to paw at the pantry, so I opened the door. She jumped up on a shelf and knocked a can of tuna to the floor. I laughed. "I see how this is going to work now. Fairchild would only help if we gave him money, and apparently, you expect tuna as payment when you decide to help me."

"Meow."

I opened the can and dumped it into a dish. "Okay. You can have the tuna, but after lunch, we get back to work. I'd love to solve both these cases, but right now, I'm most interested in finding out who is taking the current missing women. Are they dead? Being held captive? If they are being held, is there still time to save them, or at least some of them, if we figure it out early enough?"

"Meow."

"Yeah, that's a lot of questions. Even if these women are still alive, I really have no idea how we'll ever find them. We don't even know if they were ever on the islands, and even if they were brought here, if they're still here, or if the man who took them has moved them by this point. So many questions and so few answers."

Chapter 13

Tara called right after Mystique and I had finished lunch to let me know that she had received a draft of the contract from Balthazar and wondered if she could stop by to go over it with me. I told her I was happy for the company and to just come on in and come up to the third floor when she arrived. In the meantime, I decided to return to the paperwork I'd been sorting through before lunch. I really had no idea if doing all of this would net us any new information, but it was something to do on a blustery day, and I liked to feel useful even though at this moment, very little was actually required of me.

I sat down on the floor with the boxes and tried to decide which mystery to really dig into. The mystery of the missing women seemed the most relevant, but the unsolved murder of the man who had been shot as he slept was the one to grab my attention. In the end, I decided to leave it up to the cat. "Okay, so which box are we going to spend the next few hours going through?"

Mystique jumped into one of the boxes I'd left open on the floor near where I was sitting. She put her paws on the ledge, which caused the box to tumble over. Once the contents were scattered on the floor, she pushed a single sheet of paper across the room in my direction. I picked it up and looked at it. There was a name jotted down and then circled. Marley Donnelly. Marley was Aunt Maggie's best friend. Prior to Maggie marrying Michael and moving from the island, the two had owned a store named The Bait and Stitch, which sold both fishing and sewing supplies. When Maggie made the decision to marry the love of her life and move away, she'd given her half of the enterprise to Marley. I used to see Marley nearly every day, but now that Maggie was no longer around, I realized it had been months since I'd taken the time to visit with Marley.

"You want us to go and see Marley?" I asked the cat.

"Meow."

I looked back down at the sheet of paper, which seemed to contain notes relating to the shooting. "I really should stop by and say hi to her anyway. It's been much too long. Maybe she'll want to join the family for Easter like she did when Maggie lived on the island. I should ask her."

"Meow."

"I wonder why Orson had jotted down her name. I suppose Marley might have known Margaret Reynolds. Maggie and Marley would have already owned The Bait and Stitch at the time of Margaret's husband's murder. Maybe Margaret was a quilter. I suppose Orson might have been looking for information relating to the couple and any enemies they might have had." I got up and set the piece of paper on the counter. "Tara is on her way over. Once she shows me what she needs to show me, we'll go and see Marley. Since I am assuming you'll want to go, it might be best if you would continue to hang out up here so I can find you."

Mystique seemed content with that arrangement since she jumped up onto the sofa, curled up between two sofa pillows, and went to sleep.

Not long after Mystique settled in for a nap, I heard Tara's car in the drive, so I started a fresh pot of coffee to go with the muffins Tara had indicated she'd made that morning and was bringing with her.

"So does Balthazar's offer seem viable?" I asked, not really wanting to read the entire document, and not feeling that I needed to since I was certain Tara already had, and I trusted her judgment.

"More than viable. When Balthazar mentioned working out a new share agreement, I assumed he would become a partial owner, but Willow will be our new partner. Balthazar is suggesting that you and I each maintain a thirty-five percent share, and Willow would be given a thirty percent share in exchange for the dollar amount listed toward the middle of page two."

I turned to page two and looked at the number on the page. "Wow. That's very generous. I can't see any way we wouldn't be able to tear down what's there and build a brand new Coffee Cat Books."

Tara smiled. "I know. It's a lot more than I ever hoped for. Not only will we be able to rebuild, but there will be enough left over so that we can stock our inventory and have a little money in the bank as well."

"Have you spoken to Willow about this?" I asked. "She really doesn't seem to be the sort to want to accept such a large gift from anyone, and what this really comes down to is that the money Balthazar is investing is a gift to her since she's the one who will own a share of the business."

Tara nodded. "I have. I guess that between Balthazar and Alex, they managed to convince her that by accepting this gift, she will be helping us to rebuild and that without the gift, we probably will be out of business. Willow loves working at the bookstore. Even more than you do. If not for the fact that she wants to spend quality time with Barrington, I think she'd be interested in full-time work. She told me that the three days a week she spends with us mean a lot to her. I suspect that if she and Alex don't eventually marry and have children of their own, she might even be interested in working full-time once Barry is in school. But that is neither here nor there. All she's looking for at this point is three days a week, and from where I stand, I am happy to have her."

"Yeah. Me too." I looked down at the contract in my hands. "I just want to make one small change since we're changing things up anyway. We talked about giving Cassie a small share. I think you should keep your thirty-five percent so that you maintain the majority share. I'd like to give Cassie ten percent of my share."

"Are you sure? That would just leave you with twenty-five percent."

"I'm sure. Like we discussed, the bookstore is really your baby, and I would be most happy dividing my time between the bookstore and working at the newspaper with Cody. If I give Cassie ten percent, you will have thirty-five percent, Willow will have thirty, I'll have twenty-five, and Cassie will have ten. That feels right to me." I looked at Tara. "I do want to point out that even though you have the largest share, it is not in and of itself a controlling share. Theoretically, if Willow and I teamed up, we would be able to outvote you. Are you sure you are comfortable with that?"

She nodded. "I trust you both and really can't see that happening." She smiled. "When I think of the store we could build with all that extra money, I get goosebumps all up and down my arms."

"When we rebuild, we could make all those little changes we'd always talked about. I really am excited about the possibilities. If you're comfortable with this, I'm comfortable with this. I say we make the small changes to the document we discussed and then forge ahead."

Tara hugged the draft of the contract to her chest. "Okay. I'll call Balthazar and put the deal in motion."

After Tara left, I grabbed Mystique and headed downstairs to let Mr. Parsons know that the cat and I were heading to town. Francine had stopped by for tea and conversation with Mr. Parsons, and the dogs both seemed happy to spend time with them, so I left them where they were, and Mystique and I headed into town. The rain had slowed, although the sky was dark, so I suspected the break in the downpour was only a temporary situation.

In order to reach The Bait and Stitch, I had to drive by Coffee Cat Books. The place was boarded up, awaiting repair. It would be sad to see the old building that had at one time been the cannery demolished, but I did understand that a new building made more sense. Tara, Willow, Cassie, and I would need to sit down with an architect and nail down the design, but I suspected the new building would look much like the old building with a few alterations Tara and I had always wished we'd made when we remodeled the first time around.

"Cait." Marley grinned and opened her arms for a hug when I walked in with the cat trailing along behind me. "It's been much too long."

"I was just thinking that." I hugged her back.

"And who do we have here?" Marley asked as she bent over and picked the cat up.

"Her name is Mystique. She's helping me out with a few things, one of which I'd like to ask you about, but before I do, I wanted to invite you to Finn and Siobhan's for Easter dinner on Sunday."

"I'd love to come. Will Michael and Maggie be there?"

"I'm not sure. I know Mom planned to call Maggie and invite them, but I haven't heard back as of yet. Michael and Maggie have come for all the holidays since moving, so I think it's fair to assume they'll be here on Sunday as well."

"It'll be good to see them. I've barely even chatted with Maggie since Christmas." She bent over and set the cat on the floor. "Can I get you some coffee?"

"No, thanks. I've had more than enough today."

"You said you had something to ask me."

I nodded. "In the course of looking into who might have broken into the newspaper, we came across an unsolved murder from nineteen ninety-seven. It seems a man named John Reynolds was shot in the head while he slept."

"I do remember that. Let's have a seat at the quilting table, and we can chat." She looked out the front window. "With all the rain, it's been totally dead today, so I'll just lock the door and flip the sign around to let folks know I'm taking a break."

"Are you sure? If you don't want to close, we can talk in the front."

"It's fine," she said. "I haven't had a customer all day, so I've been cleaning, and to be honest, I could use a break. In fact, if you don't mind, I think I'll have my lunch while we chat. I can share my sandwich if you're hungry."

"Thanks, but Mystique and I have had our lunch. You go ahead and eat, and I'll ask my questions while you do."

I explained about the boxes of notes containing journals and other documents that Orson had left behind. I suspected that he had saved every note from every news piece he'd ever worked on. It was a lot to go through, but I also shared that Mystique seemed to have a definite opinion as to what I should be paying attention to. I showed her the piece of paper with her name on it.

"Did Orson interview you after John Reynolds died?" I asked.

"Yes. He did actually. Margaret was one of our regulars. The woman loved to sew almost as much as I do. She spent a lot of time hanging out here, and I guess you could say we became friends. Good friends."

"What sort of things did Orson ask you about?"

"He was mainly interested in the sort of relationship Margaret had with her husband."

"Sort of relationship?" I asked.

"He wanted to know if the two shared a close and intimate bond, or if there was trouble in their marriage. I told him that to the best of my knowledge, the pair had shared a happy union until about a year and a half before John's death."

"What happened a year and a half before John's death?" I asked.

"He was in an auto accident and almost died. In fact, he was in a coma for almost a week before he began to recover. According to Margaret, John was different after that."

"Different how?"

"He was harder and less affectionate. He was angry most of the time and had, on occasion, even hit both her and their son hard enough to leave a bruise. Margaret loved her husband, and she attributed the personality change to the accident. She clung to the hope that the old John would eventually return, but he never did. In fact, by the time of his death, Margaret had all but decided to leave him. Not only had the abuse been getting worse, but she was sure he was having an affair."

"Do you think Orson suspected that Margaret killed John?" I asked.

She nodded. "I suspect that was his theory, but I told him that Margaret had been making plans to take her son and move away so, therefore, had no reason to kill him. I'm not sure whether I was able to convince Orson of this fact, but I just couldn't see Margaret killing the man. Despite everything he'd done to her since the accident, she still loved him and mourned the loss of the man he'd once been."

"Was the fact that John had been abusing his wife and son a well-known fact back then?"

"No. Margaret covered it up. She didn't want him to go to prison. She wanted him to get help, which he kept promising to do, but as far as I know, never did."

"And the affair part? Had that been going on the entire year and a half since the accident?"

"Margaret wasn't sure. She did say that a few months after he was released from the hospital, he began disappearing for short periods. Usually on the weekends, which made her believe he had a woman stashed on the side. She asked him about another woman on several occasions, and he always denied it, but a woman can tell those things about the man she's sleeping with. Still, Margaret had no proof, and there were stretches where John would be home every night, so she really wasn't sure what was going on. Then about a month before John died, one of Margaret's friends saw John with another woman. They were in a bar on Orcas Island. Knowing that Margret had suspected John of being unfaithful, the friend called Margaret and told her what she'd seen. John didn't come home that night, nor did he come home the following night. When he finally did show up late on Sunday, she confronted him. He slapped her and told her that what he did with his free time was none of her business. I think that was when Margaret began to think about taking her son and leaving. She felt she needed her own proof of John's infidelity, so she hired a private detective to follow

John. The PI followed John for a couple of weeks without seeing John with this woman, and Margaret was about to give up when the detective called and told her he had a photo of John with a woman on Lopez Island. The woman in the photo was blond, and the woman the friend saw was a redhead. It was then that Margaret realized he didn't just have one woman on the side, but many. By the time the intruder broke in and shot John, Margaret had already made arrangements to leave the island forever. She hadn't even planned to tell John what she was doing. She told me she planned to pick Alton up from school and leave from there."

"And then he died."

She nodded. "And then he died. Margaret took Alton and left anyway, but she waited to bury the man, board up the house, and take care of all the little details one has to when your husband unexpectedly passes away."

I paused to take a minute to consider the situation. "Other than feeling that Margaret had a motive to kill her husband due to his abuse and unfaithfulness, did Orson seem to have any other reason for his suspicions?"

"Not that he said. And like I said, in my mind, Margaret already had a plan in place to leave the man, so why would she kill him?"

"Money?"

"John hadn't worked since the accident. He didn't have any money. Margaret had to borrow money from her sister to hire the PI. I know Orson had his suspicions relating to Margaret's involvement in her husband's death, but I really think he was wrong about this one." She paused briefly and then continued. "You know, if you want to talk to someone who might have known what was really going on, you should speak to a woman named Elliemae Crafton. She was Margaret's best friend. If Margaret was going to share her deepest thoughts with anyone, it would have been with Elliemae."

"Does she still live on the island?"

"She lives in Harthaven. I can call her if you'd like to see if she would be willing to chat with you about John and Margaret."

"That would be great. I'm not sure why this particular unsolved case has grabbed my attention, but I have to say that the more research I do, the more I'm pulled into the story."

Chapter 14

Marley called Elliemae, who was home and willing to chat with me. After Marley gave me directions to her home, I said my goodbyes, and Mystique and I headed north. By this point, the rain had stopped altogether, but the dark clouds on the horizon were heading in this direction, and I was certain that the sky would eventually open up once again and release the moisture within, so I figured I'd best make the interview a short one. I considered dropping Mystique at home, but given the approaching storm, I elected to save time by bringing her with me and leaving her in the car while I spoke to Elliemae.

Elliemae lived in a nice home in the older part of Harthaven, not all that far from the home where I'd grown up. Since Marley had called and let her know I would be arriving within the half-hour, she was waiting for me when I pulled up.

"Thank you so much for taking a few minutes to speak to me about Margaret Reynolds," I said.

"I'm not sure I'll have much to add that Marley hasn't already told you, but I'm happy to help if I can. Please come in. I have lemonade in the living room."

After she had poured a glass of the tart beverage for me, she asked what was on my mind. I shared my reason for having an interest in the case, as well as everything Marley had already shared with me. I then asked if she had anything to add.

"Not really," she replied. "It is true that John changed after the accident. It's almost like he was a different person when he woke from the coma. It's hard to explain if you hadn't known the man before and after, but if someone told me he'd been possessed while he was unconscious, I would have totally believed them."

"So John and Margaret were happy before the accident?"

"Very happy." She got up and crossed the room. She opened a drawer and took out a photo. "This is a photo of John and Margaret; it was taken just a few months before the accident. They were at a church picnic. The boy standing next to them is their son, Alton."

I looked at the photo of the handsome dark-haired man with his petite wife and equally handsome son and decided they had indeed looked happy.

"I felt so bad for Margaret after John woke up a different man than the one who'd been knocked unconscious. She really loved that man, and she tried so hard to adjust to her new circumstances and make it work, but after more than a year of putting up with his anger, aggression, and infidelity, she decided she'd had enough and made arrangements to leave the island with her son."

"And then he was shot and killed," I said.

She nodded. "Yes. Just a few days before she planned to leave. I really wish she'd gotten out of town before the madman who broke into her home decided to take out his anger in the most violent of ways. The poor thing had already gone through so much, and then to have this man she barely knew anymore but still loved, murdered while they slept. Did you know that John's blood and brain matter ended up all over poor Margaret? I really can't imagine anything worse."

"That does sound bad," I agreed. I looked down at the photo of the happy family again. "Do you know if Margaret had any idea who shot her husband?"

Elliemae shook her head. "She wasn't sure. Margaret protected John, so it wasn't widely known, but John had made a lot of enemies during the year and a half since his accident. He'd been in bar fights, and she'd recently been given proof that he'd been sleeping around with multiple women. Margaret suspected that it might have been the husband or boyfriend of one of these women who shot John. He was a handsome man, and he tended to gravitate toward young and attractive women."

"Did she know who any of these women were?" I asked.

"Initially, Margaret didn't have any names, and she hadn't even known for sure that John was being unfaithful, but then a friend of hers saw him with another woman and called and told her about it. After that, she borrowed money from her sister and hired a private detective. He was able to offer photo proof of

John's infidelity and the name of at least one of the women."

"So, she actually had a photo of one of the women?" I asked.

"Yes. She had a photo."

"Was she local? Did Margaret recognize her?"

"No. Margaret said she'd never seen the woman before. The private detective did some additional research and found out the woman actually lived in Bellingham. She was just twenty-two. I think the fact that John was cheating with a woman so much younger than she angered Margaret most of all."

"Do you know this woman's name?"

She paused, tapping her chin as she thought about it. "Susan? No, not Susan. Shawna. I don't remember her last name, but I do remember that she worked for an attorney as some sort of clerk. Margaret actually went to Bellingham to confront her and warn her to leave her husband alone."

"And did she agree to leave him alone?"

She frowned. "You know, Margaret never did share how her interview went. I'm not even sure the woman agreed to speak to her."

I handed the photo of Margaret and her family back to Elliemae. "I know you said that Margaret wasn't sure who shot her husband, but did you have a theory at the time?"

"I actually thought it might have been one of the people John was suing."

"Suing?" I asked.

"John was suing both the bartender and the owner of the bar who'd served him on the night of the accident. I guess he'd had too much to drink, which had caused him to swerve off the road in the first place, but instead of taking responsibility for his own drinking, he tried to blame everyone else."

"Did he or Margaret ever get a settlement?"

"No. The owner of the bar was able to find witnesses to testify that John had a bottle of whiskey in his car and most likely continued to drink after he left the bar. He was also able to find men and women who'd been in the bar that evening and were willing to testify that John was not too drunk to drive when he left the premises, so he must have continued to drink after he left. The lawsuit was dropped shortly before John was shot, but according to others who knew John, he wasn't giving up and had started hassling the family of the man who owned the bar. I don't know this for a fact, but it does sound like something he would do."

"You said that John was a good husband, a good father, and a good man prior to the accident. Do you have any idea why he was drinking so heavily on the night of the accident?"

Her brow wrinkled. "No. I've actually never considered that question before. It doesn't seem like the sort of thing pre-accident John would have done. I suppose John and Margaret might have had an argument or perhaps he was having problems at work. I really don't know what might have been going through his mind at the time."

"And when exactly was this accident?"

"Just before Thanksgiving. I guess it must have been November of nineteen ninety-five."

Elliemae and I chatted for a few more minutes before it started to rain. I decided I should get home before the worst of it hit, so I thanked her, then gave her my cell number, and asked her to call me if she thought of anything else. By the time I made it back to my car, the sky had really opened up. I had the feeling it was going to be a slow and precarious drive home. I slipped my key into the ignition, started the engine, and slowly pulled away from the curb. The windshield wipers were going full speed, but I could barely see where I was going. I decided to take it slow and steady, so I wouldn't run off the road. I was about halfway back to the peninsula where Cody and I lived when I decided that even slow-moving was dangerous, so I pulled over to wait it out. While I was waiting, I decided to call Finn. Something about the name Shawna rang a bell with me.

"Hey, Finn, it's Cait. Do you have a minute to look something up for me?"

"Yeah. I have a minute. What do you need?"

"If you have the list of women who went missing in the nineties on hand, can you look and see if one of the missing women was named Shawna."

"Yeah. Hang on."

He set the phone down, but I could hear him moving around in the background. I watched the sheets of water run down my windshield. I couldn't even see the landscape around me. I pretty much doubted that anyone would be driving in this, but I did find myself wondering if I'd pulled far enough off the road to avoid a collision should someone come barreling along.

"Shawna Jorgenson was the last woman to go missing in May of nineteen ninety-seven. Or at least she was the last woman on the list provided by Orson."

"Did she live in Bellingham?"

"She did."

"I think there might be something going on we haven't quite put together yet. I'm sitting in my car on the side of the road, waiting for the rain to let up enough so I can see where I'm going. Once it does, I'll head in your direction. I think the two cases Mystique has me researching might be linked in some way."

"Linked? Linked how?"

"I'll tell you everything when I get there. Are you in your office?"

"I am."

"Okay. Wait for me. I'll be there as soon as I can."

Thankfully, the rain began to slow after I had been sitting on the side of the road for about fifteen minutes. Once I felt I could see well enough to stay on the road, I started my engine and slowly pulled onto the roadway. I drove cautiously, so it took me twice as long to cover the distance between Harthaven and Finn's office in Pelican Bay than it normally did. I'd begun to wonder if Cody was out driving in this mess, which caused me to worry, so I was happy to see his truck parked in front of the newspaper when I pulled up. I debated whether or not to take a minute to go in and let Cody know I'd be next door. I figured he'd see my car and wonder where I was. I'd just picked up the cat and stepped onto the sidewalk when my phone dinged, alerting me that I had a text. It was Cody letting me know he was waiting for me in Finn's office.

Once I greeted the men, I sat down next to Cody and across from Finn, and shared everything that I'd learned from Marley and Elliemae with them. Once I had completed my retelling, I paused and asked the question that had been on my mind since my conversation with Margaret's best friend. "So the question in my mind is whether it's a clue or a coincidence that the name of the woman the private investigator photographed with John Reynolds shortly before he was shot and killed was also the name of the last victim on Orson's list."

"It does seem like quite a coincidence, given the fact that both women were from Bellingham," Cody said. "But what does that mean? Are you saying that John Reynolds was the person who was chatting up these women at various bars along Interstate 5 and then bringing them to the islands to kill them?"

"I thought Jack might be a nickname for Jackson, but it's also a nickname for John, and the timing fits," I pointed out. "Elliemae and Marley both said that John was a different person after the accident. Elliemae said that the accident happened just before Thanksgiving in nineteen ninety-five. The missing women on Orson's list started going missing in January of nineteen ninety-six, and the final woman on Orson's list to go missing was last seen in May of nineteen ninety-seven. John Reynolds was shot and killed in June of nineteen ninety-seven. Based on what we know to this point, there were no additional missing women until January of this year."

"If John is the one who was kidnapping and killing these women back in the nineties, he certainly isn't the one kidnapping them now," Finn pointed out.

"No, of course, he isn't. I guess if my theory is correct, the current kidnapper must be a copycat."

"I wonder how we can prove any of this," Cody commented. "John Reynolds is long gone, so we can't bring him in for questioning."

I nibbled on my lower lip. "I'm not sure. I guess if we can figure out who is currently kidnapping these women, assuming we're right and that actually is what's happening, once he is caught, we can ask him what he knows about John and the kidnappings in the nineties."

"This person either has access to police reports, or he knew John and knew the details of what he'd been doing, again, assuming our theory is correct. The pattern that is being repeated is very similar. Too similar," Cody pointed out, "to be a coincidence."

"Okay, say you're right," Finn said just about the same time that Mystique jumped up onto his desk. "Say it had been John who was kidnapping and killing these women. Why would someone start mimicking these killings all these years later? It has been a really long time."

"I don't know," I admitted. "There is a lot about this that doesn't make sense, but I really do feel that Mystique and I might be onto something. If nothing else, our theory seems solid enough to warrant further research."

"I agree," Finn said. "I'll see if I can find any additional proof that John was in some way linked to the missing women in the nineties. He lived on the island for quite a while. Folks knew him. If he brought these women back to the island, someone must have seen him."

"I'm pretty sure you'll find that he didn't bring the women here," I said. "Margaret's friend saw him on Lopez Island. I bet he stayed away from Madrona Island. Still, he had to be keeping these women somewhere. He must have secured rentals on the other islands. Or maybe Fairchild was correct when he said that the killer must have had a home on one of the private islands, although Elliemae said that John and Margaret were broke, so I sort of doubt that. Maybe he had a friend with a house, or maybe he knew which homes would be empty and broke in. It's really hard to say at this point."

"I'll ask around," Finn promised. "It happened so long ago that it's going to be hard to find anyone who remembers anything, but I'll try."

"In the meantime, Mystique and I will continue to work on the mystery of the current missing women. If we can figure out what is happening to these women, perhaps we can figure out what happened to the missing women in the nineties."

Chapter 15

Tara called shortly after Cody and I had returned home. The bar was closed on Mondays, so she and Danny were both off. She wondered if we had time to get together to talk about the information Danny had gathered from some of his contractor friends. I told her that she and Danny were always welcome, but I wondered if Willow shouldn't be involved in these sorts of discussions. Cassie, too for that matter. She agreed that it might be a good idea to get together when both Willow and Cassie could attend, and she admitted it was going to be hard to remember that we had new partners whose opinions would need to be considered when making any sort of decision. I suggested she call Willow to set up a time for us to meet that was convenient for her since my current schedule was pretty flexible, as was Cassie's. She agreed to my suggestion. After that, I asked her if she and Danny wanted to come over for dinner just to hang out since they were off, and she accepted the invite, saying that she felt antsy after everything that had happened and needed to get out of the house. Ten minutes later, she called me back to tell me she'd talked to Willow, who'd assured her that she was fine with us discussing the bookstore in her absence and filling her in later. The last thing Willow wanted to do, she'd assured Tara, was make anyone feel that she was interested in running things. She liked the way things had been before the explosion and wanted nothing more than to return to her regular routine. Tara had suggested we get together for lunch one day this week so we could go over everything we discussed this evening, so I called Cassie and invited her to have dinner with us. She had a date, so she declined the invitation, but at least I felt like we had attempted to reach out and include all the owners of the new Coffee Cat Books.

"It looks like the rain is still coming down pretty hard," I said after showing Danny and Tara where they could leave their wet outerwear.

"It's pouring right now, but according to my weather app, it should clear up in a couple of hours," Danny said.

"Come on upstairs," I invited. "Banjo and Summer are staying here with Mr. Parsons until the storm blows through since their little hut tends to leak, so we're going to have our meal up in our apartment rather than down here in the main dining room."

"Banjo and Summer have money. They also have a very expensive piece of land. Why don't they tear down that little shack and build a proper home?" Danny asked.

I shrugged. "I've asked them about that in the past, and they both said the shack suits them and since Mr. Parsons is happy to have their company when the weather is bad, they can just come here so why should they bother building something more suited to our oftentimes severe weather."

"To each, his own, I guess," Tara said as she started up the stairs behind Danny. "They are one of the happiest couples I know, and I guess, in the end, that's all that matters."

Danny and Tara greeted Cody, who was busy getting our dinner on the table. As if by some sort of mutual consent, none of us talked business while we ate. We discussed the weather, the cottage Cody and I planned to build, and the upcoming Easter holiday. Once we'd eaten dinner and cleared the table, we gathered in front of the fire to discuss the bookstore and the effort that would be required to rebuild and reopen.

What it really came down to was the structural integrity of the wooden supports and the amount of money it would take to repair versus tearing down and rebuilding.

"According to both contractors who looked at the place, the foundation is fine," Danny said. "If you choose to tear down the structure, you could tear up the foundation and really start from scratch, but both contractors felt that if you were willing to work with the existing footprint, you'd be able to save quite a bit of time and money. What they're both recommending is taking the building down to the studs, keeping the existing foundation, and only replacing those supports that are damaged. Doing that would limit what you could do to a degree, but how you organize the space between the supports would be up to you."

"Tara and I have always talked about how nice it would be to have the huge stone fireplace on the side wall rather than the back wall since it interfaces with the view on the back wall. Would doing a partial tear down prevent us from moving it?"

"No," Danny answered. "Not since you've converted to gas. You kept the chimney intact when you remodeled the first time, but you don't really need it. I would consider taking it out and just adding a vent to whichever wall you decide to put the fireplace on."

"And we also talked about flipping the storeroom and the office," Tara said. "The current storeroom has no windows even though one wall of the room overlooks the water."

"What you do with the interior of the structure would be up to you," Danny confirmed. "I have another friend who is an architect and is willing to work with you to draw something up. You'll want to get started right away since you'll need to obtain a permit for the new construction, and that can take a while. If you wait until summer, the wait will be even longer, so I'm going to suggest you let me set up a meeting this week."

Tara, Danny, Cody, and I discussed what we considered to be our wish list. Danny called his architect friend, who had time to meet with us on Wednesday. Tara called Willow and arranged to meet for lunch tomorrow. I texted Cassie and told her about the lunch, which she agreed to attend. That way, we could all discuss the functionality of moving the fireplace or coffee bar, which were two items Tara and I had discussed in the past.

Eventually, our conversation migrated to different topics. The return of the whales, the upcoming fishing and tourism season, the fate of the Seahawks should different trade scenarios come to pass. It had been a while since the four of us had hung out. I missed this. Since Cody and I had been living full-time with Mr. Parsons, we really hadn't entertained much. It just felt different being in someone else's home. I hoped that having the cottage would bring a feeling of normalcy back to my life. Not that we'd be there all the time. We had, after all, moved in with Mr. Parsons to help out and to keep an eye on the older man. But having the cottage with the deck I envisioned butting up to the sea, would give us a place to entertain without our guests having to tromp through Mr. Parsons' living space.

The rain had stopped by the time Danny and Tara left. In fact, the clouds had cleared, and the stars had come out. Cody and I decided to take both dogs for a walk along the beach before turning in. Banjo and Summer were watching an old movie with Mr. Parsons, and Mystique seemed perfectly content to sit in Summer's lap and watch the movie with them.

"Do you realize that this was the first time we've had guests over for dinner since we moved into Mr. Parsons' place full-time?" I asked Cody as we walked hand in hand down the beach.

"I guess I hadn't really stopped to think about it."

"We used to have people over to the cabin all the time. Inviting people over now feels different. Not that Mr. Parsons would ever complain about people having to tromp through his part of the house to get to the stairs, but in my mind, it still feels like an imposition. I'm hoping the little cottage we plan to build will serve as a place for us to entertain."

"I spoke to a contractor, and he said much the same thing Danny just said about the length of the permit process. He recommended we get started right away. When we get back to the house, maybe we can come up with a rough draft of what we are thinking. Once we have that, we can get an architect on board, and once we have plans, we can apply for the permit."

"I really hoped to have the cottage built by summer."

Cody pulled me into his arms. He leaned forward and kissed me. "I'm not sure we can get everything done we need to do before the summer building season really kicks in, but we'll do what we can. In the meantime, we'll make more of an effort to invite our friends to dinner in our apartment. It is a pretty nice apartment."

"It's a very nice apartment, and we do have that deck we never use. Maybe we should get some new patio furniture."

"I think that can be arranged. We're going to need furniture for a couple of the second-floor guest bedrooms, so I was thinking about taking a trip to Seattle. We can look at patio furniture while we're there."

"A couple of the guest rooms?" I asked.

"I guess I might have forgotten to tell you that Mom plans on bringing a friend when she comes to visit this summer."

"And will they both be staying with us?"

Cody nodded.

"When exactly is your mother coming?"

"The end of June or the beginning of July. I know that having two house guests for a month to six weeks is a lot, but…"

"But she is your mother. I get it. I really do." I leaned my head on Cody's shoulder as we continued to walk along the waterline. I loved these quiet moments when it was just the two of us. We used to take long walks all the time, but lately, it seemed as if we'd both been preoccupied and busy. I still felt the knot in my stomach that I'd been feeling for some time. I supposed that between the changes with the bookstore, the investigation into the disappearance of the missing women, the break-ins at the newspaper, and the impending visit from Cody's mother, I had reason to be stressed. Somewhere, in the back of my mind, however, I realized my feelings of doom weren't the result of any of those things, which caused me to worry about what other surprises might be waiting for me just around the corner.

Chapter 16

Tuesday, April 7

Cody had two interviews to do this morning, so I decided to stay home and continue to sort through the boxes Orson had left behind. I was still hoping to find that single clue that would break the mystery of the missing women wide open. Rambler and Max were both sleeping by the fire where they'd settled in after I'd taken them out for a short run. The rain had stopped, but it was still overcast and gloomy, which seemed to cause us all to want to settle in for a nap. Mystique was curled up on the sofa while I sat on the floor with a pile of notebooks stacked up beside me. The real problem, I decided, was that much of what Orson had written was completely illegible. At least it was illegible to me. I'm sure that he understood his unique shorthand and found it quite functional.

I'd just finished sorting through the pile of journals I'd selected to work on first and was about to get up to fetch another pile when Mystique woke up. She followed me to the stacks of boxes we'd identified as needing a second look and began to paw at the second one from the bottom of the third stack against the back wall.

"Do you want me to go through this box next?" I asked.

"Meow."

"Okay." I set the three boxes on top of the one Mystique had pointed out to the side, and carried a box with the torn cover over to rug where I'd been sitting. I refilled my coffee and sat down on the floor. I opened the box and took the stack of journals and files out, setting them on the floor beside me. I picked up the one on the top, but Mystique had other plans. She swatted at the stack until it was scattered and then pounced on a blue file folder, which she then pushed in my direction.

I picked it up. "I take it you want me to start with this one." I opened the file. There was a stack of handwritten notes inside. "Do you want me to look at anything specific?" I set the pile on the floor so the cat would have access.

"Meow." Mystique scattered the papers across the room before choosing one to bat toward me.

I picked up the page and looked at the notes. Once again, the notes were written in Orson's special shorthand. "I can't read this."

"Meow." Mystique put her paw on an address that had been circled.

"Do you want me to go here?"

"Meow." She trotted toward the door.

It was cold and windy, and I really didn't want to go out, but I'd learned a long time ago that when the cats who were here to help me decided it was time to act, it was time to act. I grabbed my coat and my backpack, called to the dogs, and headed downstairs. I stopped off in the parlor to let Mr. Parsons know where I was going and asked if the dogs could hang out with him for a while. He, of course, was happy for the company but suggested I call Finn before I drove to an address that, for some reason, Orson had associated with the case of the missing women in the nineties. I assured him that I would call Finn as soon as I determined that the address was legit, then I grabbed my umbrella from the stand and Mystique, and I headed out to my car.

The address Mystique led me toward was north of Harthaven, along a part of the shoreline where large widely spaced homes dominated. When I arrived at the indicated address and realized it did indeed exist, I hesitated. Should I call Finn? On the one hand, I didn't want him to come all the way out here for nothing. On the other hand, I wasn't a careless woman, and I had promised Mr. Parsons. Deciding to err on the side of caution, I dialed Finn's number. It went to voicemail.

"Hey, Finn, it's Cait. I'm in my car in front of a house. The address of the house is one that was in Orson's files that are associated with the missing women in the nineties, and Mystique seemed adamant that we come and check it out. I'm still in the car, so I haven't verified who currently lives here, but there is a truck with a camper shell in the drive, so I assume someone is home. I'm going to see if I can peek in any of the windows. If you get this message, call me back." I then provided the address where I was currently located in the event Finn decided a visit was warranted. Once I hung up, I slipped my phone in my pocket and then opened my car door and stepped out. I was parked along the street so as not to draw attention to myself. My plan at this point was to sneak through the trees up to the house and try to look in through the windows so I could get a feel for what I was walking into before ringing the bell.

Mystique jumped out after me, and the two of us headed toward the old and fairly rundown home. The house was in a gorgeous location. It had been built on a huge lot, probably at least an acre, and it was only yards from a private dock, which jutted out into the calm bay that curved directly into the open sea. I really wasn't sure why I'd decided that peeking in the windows before knocking on the door was the best course of action, but my gut warned me there could be danger associated with my visit, so I decided a bit of surveillance was warranted.

The first window I peeked into provided a view of an empty bedroom. I made my way to the next window and then the next until I eventually found a window that provided a view into the kitchen. There was a man in the kitchen, drinking coffee and assembling supplies he had set out on the kitchen table. The supplies included a rope, a lead plate such as the sort used with a weight bar, a very large knife, and, most noticeably, a gun. I took a step back and then faded into the woods, where I was less likely to be noticed. I recognized the man inside. His name was Alton Peyton. He was one of our suspects in the Santa bombings last December. At the time, we'd been looking for people who had reason to hate Christmas, and his name came up because his wife had left him for his best friend the previous Christmas

Eve, taking their life savings with her. Alton had spent much of this past December in bars drinking and complaining not only about his ex, but women in general.

"Alton Peyton," I whispered to myself. I looked down at the cat. "Didn't Finn say that John Reynolds full name was John Peyton-Reynolds? And wasn't his son's name Alton? I wonder if Alton simply dropped the Reynolds for some reason."

"Meow."

I glanced back toward the house, trying to put my thoughts in order. After the research we'd completed to date, we'd begun to suspect that John Peyton-Reynolds might have been the one who'd been kidnapping and killing women back in the nineties. The theorized kidnappings had stopped after he'd been shot, but they had started back up again this past January. Could it be that the son had taken up where the father left off?

I'd turned to head back to the car when Mystique took off toward the boat docked nearby.

"Mystique," I called softly so as not to alert the resident of the house to my presence. "We need to wait for Finn in the car."

The cat paused to look back at me, but then turned around and continued toward the boat. I glanced back toward the window where I'd been watching the man. I could still see movement inside, so I assumed he was continuing to do whatever it was he was doing. Making a quick decision, I followed the cat, who stepped onto the dock and then jumped onto the boat before I could stop her. My mind was telling me to leave the cat and wait in the car, which I had intended to do when I heard a noise that sounded like someone trying to scream through a gag. I'd been the one trying to scream through a gag not all that long ago, so I recognized the sound. I looked back toward the house. It appeared the man was still inside. Making a quick and probably unwise choice, I followed the cat onto the boat.

"Finn and Cody are both going to kill me," I whispered to myself as I slowly and as quietly as I could, made my way below deck. The boat was a large one, featuring a galley area toward the front of the cabin area, and a separate room, which I assumed was a bedroom, in the back. I headed toward the back of the cabin, slowly pushing the door open. "Oh, my!" I gasped when I saw the woman tied to the bed. As I'd suspected, the woman had been gagged. She started to scream and fight the ropes as I approached. "It's okay," I said. "I'm here to help you." I reached for the gag and was just inches away when everything suddenly went black.

When I woke, I was tied to the bed alongside the woman, who was now unconscious. My hands were tied, so I couldn't feel for a pulse, but based on her lack of movement, I suspected she was dead. I looked around for the cat, but she was nowhere in sight. Had she slipped away while the person who'd knocked me out and tied me up was busy with me?

I took a deep breath in through my nose. I needed to keep my wits about me. If I panicked, I was done for. I knew that because of all the other times I'd found myself caught in a tricky situation. I could see that I was on the boat I'd seen tied up near the house occupied by Alton Peyton. Based on the sound of the engine and the gentle rocking of the boat, I could tell we were no longer docked but at sea.

Well, that wasn't good. Even if I figured out a way to free myself of my restraints, where was I going to go?

I glanced at the woman tied up beside me again. She still hadn't moved, but I did think I'd noticed her chest rise and fall. Maybe she wasn't dead after all. Without being able to take a closer look, it was hard to tell.

I took a moment to calm my mind once again. I needed to focus. I needed to get both the woman tied up next to me and myself out of this. I realized my hands were tied in front of me rather than behind. Rookie mistake, I decided. I was able to bring my bound hands up to my face and pull down the cloth gag. Not that screaming would help since there was no one to hear me other than the woman who was tied up next to me and the man who'd tied us up. Still, not having the gag in my mouth allowed me to breathe easier, so I pulled it down, allowing it to hang around my neck. I wanted to toss it across the room, but I figured if I needed to, I could pull it up and play dead.

Once my gag was removed, I sat up and began to work on the rope around my ankles. When I'd been tied up at the newspaper, I'd been tied to a chair which had afforded me very little room to move around, but the kidnapper hadn't been as careful this time, and the rope around my ankles really wasn't all that tight. The rope around my wrists was going to be a problem, however, and even if I could work it loose, which I doubted, where was I going to go, or what could I do? The man I'd seen in the kitchen, the same man I assumed was piloting this boat, outweighed me by at least seventy-five pounds. Plus, I had to assume he'd brought the gun I'd seen on his kitchen table with him when he decided to take his victim and me out to sea.

The rope, the weight, and the huge knife really only led me to one conclusion. He planned to kill and weight us and then drop us into the sea where no one would ever find us unless we were lucky enough to have a shark attack us as the woman in the nineties had which had allowed her body to float to the surface. At least her family knew what had become of her. Poor Cody would never know what had happened to me. At least not for sure.

When I realized I was starting to hyperventilate, I knew I needed to stop. I wasn't going to give up quite yet. My hands were still bound, and I had no weapon or means of escape, but at least my legs were free, and the gag was off. I sat quietly and looked around the room. It was small yet functional. A bed, a small closet, and a small cabinet I assumed was used to store clothing and personal supplies. I noticed a phone charger plugged into the wall, which made me wonder if I still had my phone. I reached around to feel for it but found my pocket empty.

I could hear the man walking around upstairs. It sounded like there was just one person on board other than the woman and me. I supposed as long as I could hear the engine, I could assume he was up on the deck, which gave me a bit of leeway to come up with a plan. Maybe there was something down here I could use to contact someone. Perhaps a radio. I was about to get up off the bed when the engine died. My instinct was to run and hide; I was so traumatized that I didn't realize there was nowhere to run. The woman on the bed moved her legs, which at least confirmed she was still alive. Maybe the man who was taking us out to sea had just cut the engine to check on us. Maybe we weren't out of time. I realized my best bet was to pretend I'd never even come to, so I draped the rope around my ankles so it would appear they were still tied, pulled the gag into my mouth, then laid back down and closed my eyes. When I heard the man enter the room, it was nearly impossible not to thrash around, but I willed myself to stay completely still, and somehow I was able to do just that.

I heard him moving around the room. My heart was pounding, and I was having a hard time keeping my breath steady. I thought he was going to leave, but just when I thought it was safe to open my eyes, I felt a weight on the bed. I knew I needed to lay still, but I couldn't help myself. My eyes opened against my will, and I found myself staring into the dark brown eyes of the man I was sure planned to kill me.

"Ah, I see you're awake."

I didn't answer or move. The gag was still in my mouth, and I didn't want to give away the fact that my legs were free quite yet.

"It's a pity you didn't mind your own business. You reporter types are always sticking your noses into things that don't concern you."

The man stood up and began doing something behind me that I couldn't see. I wondered if the other woman had regained consciousness as well. Even though I'd seen her legs move, if this was going to be our time to die, I found myself wishing she was already dead to save her from the terror and pain I predicted was ahead of us.

"I should have hit you harder and been done with it that day you walked in on me at the newspaper. At the time, I chose to be merciful, but I can see that choice only led to problems down the line. I know you can hear me, so just so you know, I am going to finish things today the way I should have then."

At this point, I couldn't help myself. I reached up and pulled down my gag. "Why? Why did you break into the newspaper? Why are you going to kill me? Why have you been killing women for the past few months? Is it because of what your father did? Did you know about that?"

I sat up and looked directly at him. I didn't suppose acting dead was going to save me, so I might as well try to stall him. Maybe Finn had gotten my message and had figured out what had happened. Maybe Finn was on his way to rescue me, and I only needed to delay being plunged into the sea until he got here.

"You really are forever the reporter, aren't you? Here you are, about to die, and you spend your last minutes interviewing me rather than pleading with me for your life. The others pleaded with me, you know. I guess that's why I chose them. They seemed the helpless sorts, but you, you're different. I actually feel bad about what I am going to do to you."

"So appease my curiosity before you kill me," I said. "Why did you break into the newspaper?"

"I broke in to find Orson's notes. He knew everything, but I imagine you've figured that out by now. He knew what my father had done, and he knew what my mother had done."

"Your father killed at least thirteen women in seventeen months. He'd pick them up in a bar along the Interstate, promise them a weekend on the islands, kill them, weight them, and dump them in the sea. I did figure that out. But your mother? What exactly did your mother do?"

"She killed my father. Shot him in the head while he slept. I figured you'd realize that by now."

"Your mother shot your father? Why? I heard she had plans to leave him."

He began tying the rope he'd brought to a weight. "She did plan to leave him, but when she somehow figured out what my father was doing, she knew she could never be happy if he was still here on the island, killing women, so she killed him."

I frowned. "Why? Why didn't she just call the sheriff and have him arrested? Why kill him?"

He shrugged. "I think she was trying to protect me. She was concerned about how it might affect me to have to live with the knowledge that my father was a serial killer. She was afraid his legacy would haunt me for the rest of my life. So she killed the man, called the police and reported a break-in, and then acted the grieving widow role when she buried him. Once that was taken care of, she boarded up the house, packed us up, and moved three thousand miles away."

"But you figured it out?"

"I did. When I shared the fact that I planned to move back to Madrona Island with her, she was overly upset by my decision. She reminded me over and over that my father had been murdered on this island and that moving back to the island would bring me nothing but nightmares and heartache. That caused me to wonder about the depth of her resistance, so I began to poke around in the details surrounding my father's death."

"And you figured out what happened."

"It's more that I remembered what happened. I guess with all the trauma, I'd forgotten, but once I began to really think about it, things began to come back to me."

"I heard you weren't home when your father was shot."

"I wasn't. My mother had arranged for me to spend the night at a friend's house, but I was there when Orson came to the house to speak to my mom. I'd been hiding in the closet, playing a game, so they weren't aware of my presence. Orson had figured out that it had been my father who was kidnapping and killing young women, and he suspected that she'd figured it out and killed the monster who'd taken over his husband's body while he laid unconscious in a coma."

"So, your mother actually believed your father was possessed by a demon?"

He picked up the knife and ran a finger along the blade. That almost caused me to scream, but I managed to swallow it down. I knew stalling was my only hope.

"She did believe that. In her mind, it wasn't the man she'd loved and married she killed, but the demon who'd stolen his life. Orson seemed to believe that as well, so by the end of the conversation, they agreed that she would take me and leave, and he would bury what he'd found."

I supposed that explained a lot. "So, why did you decide to pick up where your father left off?"

He held the knife to my throat as if measuring it to make sure it would suffice. I gasped but was able to hold back the scream.

"Why?" I asked again.

He took a step back. "I guess maybe this demon is the sort to be passed along the bloodline. I'm not sure how it works, but once I'd gotten over the hurt and devastation of my wife leaving me for my best friend, the anger set in. I didn't set out to become a serial killer, but in the end, that's what happened. It was all quite by accident."

"Accident? How do you accidentally go to Seattle, kidnap a woman, bring her back here, kill her, and dump her in the sea?"

"I didn't set out with that course of action in mind. It was around Christmas time. I'd been drinking a lot, and the bartenders at the local bars were getting tired of the bar fights I'd been starting, so they'd banned together and stopped serving me. I decided that a change of scenery would be nice, so I took the ferry and ended up in Seattle. I met a woman at a bar, and she seemed interested in the fact that I lived on Madrona Island. I found myself inviting her back to the house, figuring I could lose myself in this woman until the pain of the holiday passed, but by the time I was done with her, I realized I still wasn't satisfied, so I slit her throat. Talk about a rush. I'd really never felt anything quite as wonderful as I felt watching the life drain from this woman. I remembered what I'd learned from my father, so I weighted and dumped the body in the sea." He smiled as if remembering a fond memory. "She was my first. I've had others since, but she'll always hold a special place in my heart."

"You really are sick."

He grinned. "Yes, I guess I am." He walked around the bed and picked up the woman next to me. She started to struggle. When he grabbed the knife, I was certain he was going to slit her throat, which caused me to lunge toward him, effectively giving away any advantage I might have had by him not knowing my legs were free. I rammed into him with the full weight of my body, which caused him to drop the woman at his feet. He turned, reached into his bag, and pulled out a gun. He aimed it directly at my head. "You are a tricky one, aren't you?"

"You won't get away with this. Finn is onto you. It's only a matter of time until he proves what you are up to."

"I realize that. I guess I'll need to head south once I dump the two of you. Mexico is lovely this time of the year."

He lifted the gun and started to pull the trigger when Mystique seemed to fall from the sky, landing on his head. I guess she might have been up in the overhead storage area. The man jerked to dislodge her, and the gun went off, but the bullet missed me and hit the wall behind me. Alton grabbed for the cat, who was scratching at his eyes and face, dropping the gun as he did so. I scooted forward and grabbed the weapon. My wrists were still tied, but my legs were free, so I was able to stand up. It took what seemed like a long time for him to get the cat off him, but it was probably only seconds. It was long enough, however, for me to gain the advantage.

"Don't move," I said, pointing the gun at his chest.

He looked crazed with rage as he lunged toward me. I closed my eyes and pulled the trigger.

Chapter 17

Sunday, April 12

As I sat with my large extended family, watching the kids in the choir sing their hearts out on Easter Sunday, I found myself thanking God that both myself and the woman who'd been tied up next to me had lived to spend this special day with those we loved. The shot I'd managed to get off had injured but not killed Alton Peyton. After he'd fallen to the floor, I'd been able to grab his phone and call Finn who'd received my earlier message and was already out on the water looking for me.

Alton was in custody, awaiting trial on multiple murder charges. He'd been offered some sort of deal in exchange for a confession detailing everything he knew about his father's murders as well as his own. He was going to spend his life behind bars, there was no question about that, but I guess in exchange for his cooperation, he was to be afforded certain luxuries like cigarettes and additional yard time.

He also shared with Finn the details, as he knew of them, of his mother's involvement in his father's death. Finn passed that information along to the FBI, who did some digging and found out that Alton's mother had passed away a little over six months ago.

"The kids did such a good job," Siobhan said to me after mass. "That last song brought tears to my eyes."

"They did get it just right," I agreed. "I have to admit I was somewhat worried given the complexity of the number, but they really came through."

"They really did. Finn and I are going to head back to the house since I have a few things to do before everyone arrives for dinner." She hugged me. "I just wanted to say again how happy I am that you are here with us this Easter."

"I'm happy about that as well," I smiled.

Siobhan turned to leave, and then she turned back around. "Are you doing okay? Emotionally, I mean. What you went through had to have been traumatic."

"I'm fine. Really. Now go home and do what you need to do. Cody and I will be by with Mr. Parsons in an hour or so."

She hugged me again. "Okay. See you in a bit."

When we arrived home, Mr. Parsons was dressed in his Sunday clothes and ready to go. Mystique, who seemed to have settled in with Mr. Parson and showed no signs of leaving us anytime soon, was curled up in the parlor with both dogs. I'd decided to leave the animals here at the house since so many people had ended up being invited, but I figured if the party went on too long, Cody and I could take a break to see to the dogs.

"It's nice that it's such a lovely day and everyone is able to enjoy the outdoors," I said to Siobhan, after joining her in the kitchen.

"It's a perfect day," she agreed. "It does my heart good to have everyone together again. Well, everyone other than Aiden. I do find I'm missing him today."

"Yeah," I agreed. "Me too." I glanced out the window. "Connor is having a blast with Barry. They really are at a fun age."

"They really are," Siobhan agreed. "Mom and Gabe came over last night and helped Maggie, Michael, Finn, and I hide eggs. Connor was excited when he woke up to find that the Easter Bunny had been here. When Cassie came by for breakfast, he spent the entire time she was here telling her all about it."

"I'm sorry I missed it."

She opened the refrigerator and took out the potato salad. "You'll have your own little ones to enjoy an egg hunt with soon enough. Can you stir the beans?"

I did as she asked. "I'm not really sure about that, but I am enjoying viewing the holiday through the eyes of my nephew." I glanced out the window. Mr. Parsons, Balthazar, Francine, Summer, and Banjo were sitting in lawn chairs being entertained by Connor and Barry, who seemed intent on showing them every egg in their baskets. Mr. Parsons seemed to be enjoying the attention, but I did wonder how he would feel about things if Cody and I did decide to bring a child into his home. I supposed he'd be fine with it. He did, at times, talk about Cody and me having a family.

"So are Tara and Danny living together?" Siobhan asked. "They really seem to be in an *on-again* phase in their relationship, which made me wonder. I asked Danny, but he was noncommittal. I figure that Tara might have talked to you about it."

"I did ask her about it, and she said that they haven't done anything formally, but he does spend the night at her place pretty much every night, so it's probably just a matter of time."

"Are you worried?"

I paused and held up the spoon I'd been stirring beans with. "I was at first, but I spoke to Tara, and she seems certain that things will work out this time. I really hope they do. I want that for both of them."

"Yeah, me too." Siobhan took down a bowl for the coleslaw she'd made earlier and refrigerated. "They've been through so much together. I really hope they find their light at the end of the tunnel. I guess if Danny and Tara do eventually marry, we'll just have Aiden to work on."

"What about Cassie?" I asked.

"She's just a baby. She has time to find Mr. Right. But Aiden, he's getting on in years. I really do fear that if he doesn't find someone soon, he never will. I want for him what Finn and I and you and Cody have. I want him to find his other half to grow old with."

"Yeah," I agreed. "That would be nice. I guess these things tend to work themselves out on their own timeline."

"Speaking of timelines, last night, Maggie told me that she and Michael are thinking about moving back to the island."

I raised a brow. "Really?"

She nodded. "The only reason they moved in the first place was because they felt it would be easier after Michael decided to leave the priesthood to marry her. When we talked, she told me that enough time had passed and people had gotten used to the idea of the two of them being together, so she thought it might be okay."

"She doesn't want her house back, does she?"

Maggie had gifted the house she'd inherited from her father to Siobhan when she'd married Michael and moved away.

"No. She assured me that was the furthest thing from her mind. Actually, there's a house for sale on the water near where Mom and Gabe live. They went and looked at it yesterday and plan to go for a second look tomorrow."

"Wow. That is wonderful news. I've really missed having her around. I hope it works out."

She picked up the plate with the sliced ham and grilled ribs. "Yeah, me too. She's part of our family. She should be here with us so she can be an everyday part of our children's lives."

"Do you need help?" Cassie asked after walking in from the yard.

"I'm ready to start putting the food out," Siobhan said. "But first, as long as I have both of my sisters here at the same time, I have something to tell you."

"Is everything is okay?" I asked.

"Everything is great. Finn and I plan to announce this to the group when we pray before dinner, but I wanted the two of you to know first."

"Know what?" Cassie asked.

"Come this November, Connor will be getting a younger brother or sister."

As I hugged Siobhan, I glanced out the window behind her. Almost everyone I loved had gathered together on this special day. There were times when life was trying, but deep in my heart, I knew that even if I had a chance to do so, I wouldn't change a single thing.

NEW From Kathi Daley Books

Summerhouse Reunion –
https://amzn.to/3btaroM
Topsail Sundays – https://amzn.to/2ULHU79
Campfire Secrets - https://amzn.to/39Tm07O

Preview of Summerhouse Reunion

Sometimes life is about letting go. Letting go of the way things were supposed to have been. Letting go of unmet dreams and incomplete plans. Letting go of the anger that consumes you as you struggle to make sense of an unfinished life. I'd spent the last year denying the inevitable, negotiating for a different ending, screaming to the heavens that it wasn't supposed to happen this way, and finally struggling to accept an ending that should never have been.

Letting go, I realized somewhere along the way, was the hardest thing I'd ever had to do.

"It's a beautiful day." A woman with white hair walked up beside me as the spray from the rough sea misted my face.

"Yes." I turned and smiled. The woman looked to be a few years older than my sixty-eight-year-old mother; unlike my mother, however, who simply could not or would not understand the grief that haunted my every waking moment, this woman looked at me with compassion and understanding. "It's a little rougher than I like my ferry rides, but beautiful all the same. My name is Kelly. Kelly Green. I'm afraid I can't immediately place you, but I feel like we've met."

"We have met, although it has been a long time since we've seen each other. About twenty years, to be more specific."

My brows shot upward. "Dottie Pemberton?"

The woman smiled and offered her hand.

"Wow." I reached out and hugged the woman. "I'm so sorry I didn't recognize you. It's just that…"

"It's just that the fifty-two-year-old woman you remember looked a bit differently from the seventy-two-year-old woman standing before you today."

"Yes." I stepped back. "I mean, no. I mean, sure, your hair is different, and I guess we all have a few more laugh lines, but still…" I realized I was rambling, so I stopped and hugged the woman again. "How are you?"

"I'm as well as can be expected. I was sorry to hear about Kayla."

My smile faded just a bit. The death of my twin sister and best friend still hurt almost more than I could bear. I'd tried to do as others seemed to want and hide my pain, but no matter how hard I tried, the simplest thing—a song, a scent, a memory—would remind me just how much I'd lost, and the grief would return in a wave that would envelop me and then cast me into a sea of darkness once again.

"I guess it must have been extra hard with her in a coma for so long and not knowing how things would work out in the end," Dottie added after a moment.

She had no idea. In reality, Kayla had died a year ago, when a distracted driver had slammed into the car she was driving, but while everyone assured me that her mind was gone, her body had lived on, and as long as she clung to life, I'd clung to hope. Then, two months ago, her distraught husband decided to pull the plug and let her go peacefully, and I knew that my life would never be the same.

"How've you been holding up?" Dottie asked. She looked concerned, which I supposed was understandable because I hadn't said a word since the moment she'd brought up Kayla's name. "I do understand how difficult something like this can be. I suppose it is even possible to lose ourselves in our grief."

I cringed as I remembered the random acts of craziness that had been brought on by my overwhelming grief. "It has been hard," I finally said. "But I'm hanging in there. Some days are harder than others. Some days it doesn't seem real. But I guess you might understand that. I heard your Harold passed away as well."

"Yes. Three years ago. He was the love of my life, and I miss him every day."

I squeezed her hand. "I'm so very sorry. Sometimes I think Kayla's death would have been easier to deal with if she'd lived a good, long life before passing. Forty-two is much too young. She had so many things yet to do. She had a husband and two daughters who needed her, and she had me, who probably needed her most of all. But then I stop and ask myself if her passing would have been easier if she'd been seventy or eighty or a hundred, and I can't help but be faced with the truth—when you lose half of your heart, it is going to hurt no matter how long you've had together on this earth."

"It is true that losing someone you love is never easy. How are her husband and daughters holding up?"

I thought about the husband and daughters left behind. "It's been hard, but the girls are in college now and live busy lives. The accident did occur a year ago, so I guess you could say they've had time to adjust. Mark was a mess in the beginning, but he seems to have moved on. He's even dating." I exhaled slowly. "Truth be told, I'm really the only one who hasn't been able to let go. Everyone says I should. Everyone says the time for grieving has passed. But losing Kayla feels like losing half my soul."

Dottie smiled in understanding but didn't respond. She turned to watch a pair of dolphins who'd decided to race the ferry, or at least it seemed as if that was what they were doing. I took a moment to rein in my emotions. They still felt so raw, I couldn't quite shake the feeling that a huge cosmic mix-up had occurred, and Kayla wasn't meant to die. Not only was she much too young, as I'd pointed out to whatever celestial body might be listening, but in dying, she'd broken a promise, and Kayla was the sort to take any promise she made quite seriously.

A small black bird landed on the railing, not far from where I was still standing next to Dottie. I closed my eyes as I let my mind transport me back in time. I felt the tension fade just a bit as the years fell away, and I conjured up a happier time. I thought about the two little girls who'd looked just the same. Two little girls who were not only sisters but best friends and soulmates as well. I remembered the promise made by those little girls, and I grieved for the hope that had been shattered when that promise was ultimately broken.

When Kayla and I were kids, I guess around six or seven, a friend of ours lost both her parents in an airplane accident. The tragedy was too great for either of us to understand, and I remember that we'd both had nightmares for weeks. The content of our dreams was somewhat different, but the subtext was much the same. We both dreamed of a dramatic event that would rip us from the life we loved, only to be thrust into an empty space, where we'd find ourselves lost and alone.

One night, long after we were supposed to be asleep, Kayla came into my room and climbed into my bed. She was shaking and crying, so I held her close while she shared the depths of the terror she'd been feeling since our friend had been orphaned. I'd been feeling it as well, but I wanted to comfort my sister, so I reminded her that no matter what happened, even if our parents died and we were left alone in the world, we'd always have each other. That reminder seemed to help both of us, so we'd made a pact that we'd always be there for each other, no matter what. We'd even promised to die on the same day, so neither of us would ever have to be alone. As absurd as that might sound, I think there might be a tiny part of me that was angry with Kayla for not upholding her part of the promise.

"So, what brings you to Shipwreck Island after all these years?" Dottie asked after a while.

I tucked a lock of long blond hair that had blown across my face behind my ear before answering. "Carrie Davidson invited me. I guess she had the idea of getting the whole gang together for a long-overdue reunion."

"So Quinn and Nora are coming as well?"

I nodded. "They are. Carrie rented the summerhouse my family used to own for five weeks."

"Five weeks. That's quite the vacation."

"I'm not sure I'll stay for the entire period, but I did promise to show up and see how it went. Honestly, I may not have made the effort at all, but this year is the twenty-fifth anniversary of the summer Peggy went missing, and Carrie wanted to do something to commemorate the role she played in our lives." I turned slightly as a seagull landed on the railing beside me, chasing away the small black bird that had occupied the space. "It's not that I don't want to remember her; it's more that I'm afraid my already raw emotions aren't going to be able to endure yet another reminder of what has been lost."

"I remember you were close."

"The closest. She was like a sister to us, and we never really had the chance to say goodbye. Given the fact that she simply disappeared and no one ever knew what had happened, her family never did hold a funeral. I guess they never gave up hope that she'd find her way back to them."

Dottie didn't respond, but I could tell that I had her full attention.

"Carrie thought it would be nice to have a small ceremony," I continued. "Nothing formal. I think it will be just the four of us."

"I guess it's been quite a while since the four of you have been on the island at the same time."

I nodded. "I was here for Carrie and Carl's fifteenth anniversary party almost five years ago, but Kayla was on a cruise with her husband, so she didn't make it, and Quinn was overseas doing a story, so she didn't make it either. Kayla and I came for our birthday when we turned thirty, but Nora was in Europe, and Quinn was in Africa, so I think the last time we were all on the island together was for Carl and Carrie's wedding. Wow, I had no idea it had been almost twenty years since we'd all been together." Where had the time gone? "Of course, now that Kayla is gone, I guess we can never all be together again."

My heart tightened as I thought of the six little girls who lived different lives but reunited each and every year when our families returned to their summer homes. Carrie's family lived on the island year round, but Quinn, Nora, Peggy, and Kayla and I lived elsewhere during the school year. I remembered how much I'd looked forward to summering on the island. Those summers were some of the best times of my life.

"I ran into Carrie at the market a few months ago. She's lost a lot of weight," Dottie informed me, changing the subject, which was very much appreciated given my fragile emotional state. "I'd wondered if she might be ill, but her mother told me that Carl had filed for divorce, and Carrie wasn't dealing with things all that well. I guess I don't blame her. I can't imagine having the man you loved and planned to spend your life with decide that he preferred to spend his life with someone else."

"It has been difficult for her," I agreed. "I've chatted with her on the phone on a regular basis since Carl left, and she just seems so lost. I suppose it's even worse when Jessica is away at college, and poor Carrie is living in that big, old house all alone. I suggested to her that she should sell the house and buy something smaller, but I think there has been a part of her that's held on to the hope that Carl would come to his senses and return one day. Of course, now that the divorce is finalized, I guess she doesn't even have that to hang on to."

"I don't know Carl well, but based on what I do know, I think Carrie might be better off without him. I'd noticed him noticing other women for years."

I hated to admit it, but I'd noticed the same thing almost since the day the two married. "I couldn't agree more," I voiced. "Carrie really is better off without Carl, although I would never say that to her. I think she is still at the point where she is totally focused on what she's lost and is not of the mind to consider what she may have gained with Carl's departure."

Dottie shielded her eyes from the sun as the ferry turned toward the island. "I ran into Ryder just last week, and he said pretty much the same thing. Based on what I've heard from others on the island, he's been her rock through this whole ordeal."

I smiled at the memory of Carrie's little brother. "Ryder always did have his sister's back, even though he was younger. Carrie told me he's the mayor now."

"Yes, and a darn good one he is. Much better than Mayor Hadley, may he rest in peace."

I crossed my arms on the railing and looked out to sea. "I'm having a hard time picturing Ryder as mayor. When we were kids, he was such a pest and always in trouble. In fact, I think he was voted most likely to end up in prison by his senior class."

Dottie chuckled. "He does have a colorful past, and he still tools around town on that Harley of his, but in my opinion, he has done more to bring growth and prosperity to the island than any of his predecessors. The boy might wear his hair a bit too long, and I'm not overly fond of the leather jacket he seems so attached to, but Ryder has vision, and he's a hard worker. He has a promising future ahead of him."

"Has he kept his veterinary practice open?"

"He has. Being mayor in a small town like Hidden Harbor is more of an honorary title than a source of income, so all our mayors have had day jobs. Ryder is still very committed to the animals he cares for, but now he is committed to the people of the island as well."

I shook my head as I tried to picture Ryder West all grown up. I hadn't run into him during my last two visits to the island, but I had seen him briefly at Carl and Carrie's wedding almost twenty years before. Even then, he'd showed up in a leather vest and leather pants rather than the tux Carrie had picked out for him. Of course, he'd only been seventeen at the time, which meant he must be thirty-seven by now. I had to admit that most people matured quite a bit in the years between seventeen and thirty-seven.

"I guess you heard that Sheriff Renshaw retired after serving the community for forty years," Dottie continued.

"No, I hadn't heard," I said, raising a brow. "I guess I should have expected as much. He must be well into his sixties now."

"Sixty-nine. He first started working in law enforcement when he was just twenty-five, and he retired two years ago. He was a good man and a good cop who has been missed, although Sam Stone has done an excellent job as well since he took over the role."

"Sam Stone is the sheriff?" I had to admit I was even more surprised to hear that than I had been to hear that Ryder West was now the mayor. I seemed to remember that Sam was two years older than I was, so I supposed he must be around forty-four by now. As a teen and young adult, he was very much a wild child, but as I'd already told myself once in the past five minutes, people did tend to change. "I think the last time I saw him was at Carl and Carrie's wedding as well. I remember that he'd been traveling with a rock and roll band and was getting ready to head out on tour."

"He did leave the island for almost a decade, but then he came back about ten years ago and joined the force as a deputy. He is a hard worker who is well-liked and highly regarded on the island, so when Renshaw decided to retire, he recommended Sam as his replacement. In my opinion, the lad has done an excellent job filling the very big shoes Renshaw left when he decided to move to Oklahoma."

"Sheriff Renshaw moved to Oklahoma?"

She nodded. "I guess he has kin there."

I looped my arm through Dottie's. "You know, when I boarded this ferry, I had very mixed emotions about returning to Shipwreck Island and Hidden Harbor, but after chatting with you about the people I left behind, I find that I am very much looking forward to becoming reacquainted with the men and women who were such a huge part of my life as a child." I paused to remember the fun Kayla and I'd had every summer when we were children. The friends we'd made, the trips we'd taken, and the little skip we'd used to learn to sail. "Does Old Man Brewster still run the marina?"

Dottie chuckled. "The old geezer is still policing the fishing boats, the same as he always has."

"To be honest, I'm surprised he is even still alive. I seem to remember him being about a hundred when I was a kid."

"Brew has lived his life in the sun, so he looked weathered and aged even when he wasn't all that old. I think he is about eighty-five now. But he is a young eighty-five. Not only does he have the energy of a man half his age, but he is just as ornery as he ever was."

I grabbed onto the railing as the ferry made a sharp turn. I could see the island in the distance and suspected we'd be docking within the next twenty minutes. "One of the things I really love about Shipwreck Island is the fact that, while many leave within a few years of moving there, those who stay tend to stay for the duration."

"That's true. We do have our share of old-timers. Of course, with the bump in tourism that we've seen in the last decade, the number of young families moving to the island has grown significantly as well. I guess you must have noticed all the new housing when you were here five summers ago."

"Actually, my trip five years ago was a quick one. I came over on the ferry on Friday afternoon, attended the anniversary party Saturday, and then went home on Sunday. I didn't have the time or opportunity to really look around."

"Well, you'll need to take the time during this visit. I think you will be surprised at the changes to both sides of the island in the last ten years."

A voice came over the loudspeaker announcing that the ferry was preparing to dock.

"It's been really good catching up with you, but it sounds like we should head down to the car deck. Let's do lunch while I'm on the island," I suggested.

"I'd like that very much."

"Do you have a cell? I can text you my number."

Dottie nodded. "I do have a cell, but I left it in the glove box of my car. If you text me your number, I'll text you back, and we can arrange something."

She recited her number, and I added her to my contacts and texted my number to her right then and there. I knew from prior experience that if I didn't do it now, I'd most likely forget all about it. We both decided to head down to the car deck, so we chatted as we climbed down the steep stairway to the lower level.

Once the ferry docked, I got in line and followed the cars onto Shipwreck Island. The island was surrounded by deep water that allowed even the largest ships to pull right up to the docks that had been built in key locations over the years. Prior to the island being inhabited, the area had seen more than its share of shipwrecks. Based on what I remembered of local history, there had been more than one cargo ship heading up the coast that had failed to see the landmass in the fog and plowed right into it. Of course, now every ship had sonar, GPS, and various other warning systems. Additionally, the island currently boasted six lighthouses, so it had been at least a century since the island had claimed any new victims.

There were two main towns on the island, which was conveniently located off the coast of Central California. Sea Haven was on the east side of the island and closest to the ferry terminal, while Hidden

Harbor was on the west side and accessible only by sea or a narrow road that climbed up over the mountain at its center. Due to the small size of the island, the mountain acted as a natural barrier that tended to keep the two communities separate.

The drive up and over the mountain was gorgeous. The meadows were green and dotted with wildflowers, and the rivers ran full after the steady spring rain. When Kayla and I were children, our family lived in San Francisco, where our father worked as a business banker, and our mother ran a charitable foundation. Both our parents worked a lot of hours, but every June, as soon as school let out, our parents would close up the house in Pacific Heights, and we'd all pile into the van to make the trip to Shipwreck Island for the summer. Mom had a busy social life on the island, and Dad continued to work remotely, but the time we spent in the summerhouse as a family was priceless in my mind.

As I arrived at the summit of Sunset Mountain, I could see the town of Hidden Harbor tucked into the harbor for which it was named. Hidden Harbor was settled by rich families from the city, so although the area was remote, the town and the homes surrounding it reflected the opulent lifestyle of its upper-class residents. As I wound my way down the narrow mountain road, I found my anxiety level increasing with each passing mile.

I really was excited about seeing my friends, but the idea of staying in the same house where I'd spent summers with Kayla left me feeling agitated in a way I couldn't quite explain. When Carrie had first invited me to the island, I assumed she was inviting me to stay with her in her large home, but after I accepted the invite, she'd sprung it on me that she needed to get away from the walls she felt were closing in on her and had rented the same beachside home my family used to own. While she admitted to feeling better about the choice of location for our reunion, the thought of spending time in the home where I'd once been so happy almost caused me to hyperventilate.

I would admit, however, that the summer home my father designed was pretty awesome. Set on one of the nicest beaches on the island, the views were amazing from every window. When I'd lived there as a child, the home featured four bedrooms and five baths, but the investor who'd purchased the house from my mother after my father's death had converted the huge suite on the third floor into two, still large but smaller suites.

The second floor of the home featured three bedrooms, all with private balconies overlooking the sea, while the first floor housed a huge kitchen, formal dining and living areas, family and game rooms, two bathrooms, an office, and laundry facilities.

The town of Hidden Harbor, often referred to as the village, was elegant but compact. The village was located behind the harbor, which I supposed made sense because rich men and women who docked their yachts in the harbor for a few days could simply walk into the small commercial area that featured upscale shopping, elegant restaurants, and eclectic bars.

I slowed as I approached the outskirts of the town. I knew I'd need to watch for a fork in the road. The village was to the left, while the summerhouse of my youth was to the right. I wasn't entirely certain when Carrie planned to arrive, but it was a beautiful, sunny day, so I supposed that if I got to the house first, I'd take a walk along the beach while I waited for her.

"It looks just the same," I whispered to Kayla as I turned onto the coast road and headed north. "The white sand beach, the sapphire blue sea, the rolling waves, and the endless sky. All of it exactly as we remembered."

My mother hated it when I talked to Kayla, insisting that I really did need to find a way to let her go, but I knew in my soul that I would never let go of this relationship with the sister who shared my heart.

"I'm excited to see the gang, but I'm also terrified that I won't be able to handle the memories created by staying in the same house where we lived as children. God, I wish you were here. I wish you could see what I see and feel what I feel. I wish we could sit and chat late into the night the way we used to."

I wiped a tear from my cheek and forcefully steered my thoughts toward something a bit less emotional. As I drove farther toward the north shore of the island, the empty space between the homes increased, giving the area a desolate feel. Many residents moving to the island wanted to be closer to town, which meant the farther from town you traveled, the more sparsely populated the beachfront property became. The house my family used to own was the last one on the coast road. I didn't know if anyone had built on either side of it since I'd last visited, but when I was a child, the house stood alone along the northernmost point of the white sand beach.

After arriving at my destination, I stopped to consider the house. It had been a pale yellow when we'd lived there. Now it was sky blue. I liked it. The shutters had been painted a dark gray that contrasted nicely with the white trim, and there was a white screened-in porch. It looked as if someone had installed a new roof as well. The silver Mercedes in the drive informed me that Carrie had arrived. I wasn't sure if I was happy or sad about that, but it was what it was, so I opened the door of my Porsche and stepped out into the drive.

"Kelly!" Carrie yelled as she ran out of the house and onto the drive. "I can't believe you're actually here."

"I can't believe it either." I hugged her back.

She pulled away just a bit. "Let me look at you. It's been so long, but you look just the same."

I smiled. "I don't know about that, but I will admit that I haven't updated my look in ages." I dug my fingernails into my hand to stop the tears pooling in the corners of my eyes. "You look fabulous and so different. I guess you went the opposite route and changed everything."

She laughed. "Divorce will do that to you. After Carl left, I looked in the mirror and decided I wanted to change everything about myself. I lost thirty pounds, bleached my brown hair blond, cut it short, and even got blue contacts. Now, when I look in the mirror, I no longer see the frumpy, outdated woman Carl couldn't wait to replace, but a new woman he most definitely would have looked twice at had we not already been married."

I supposed I understood why Carrie might want an entirely new look after her husband of twenty years dumped her for a younger woman, but when *I* looked in the mirror, I saw not only my old, familiar image but Kayla as well. I knew that I would cling to that for as long as I could and wouldn't change a single thing about my look, no matter how outdated my long hair and simple style became.

"Grab your stuff, and we can choose rooms," Carrie said. "Personally, I think the two of us should settle into the two larger suites on the third floor. Initially, I felt greedy claiming one of the larger suites as my own, but then I remembered that I was the one who did all the planning for this event, so I deserved one of the larger suites."

"I agree. You do deserve one of the larger suites." I thought about my old bedroom on the second floor, and the Jack and Jill bathroom that connected my room to Kayla's. Part of me wanted to stay in my old room, but another realized that taking a room on the newly remodeled third floor would be a lot easier on my emotions. "And I'll take the second of the two third-floor suites, as you suggested. I always wished my bedroom, rather than my parents, was up there when I was a kid."

After we stowed my luggage in the suite, we headed out onto the back deck that overlooked the sea. Carrie poured us each a glass of wine, which I welcomed after the emotional day I'd had to this point. It would be good to relax with old friends. Maybe by visiting the past, I could begin to heal in the present.

"I've been struggling with what to say or not say about Kayla," Carrie said once we'd settled in with our wine. "I'm sure you must be hurting, and part of me feels like it might be easiest for you if everyone just avoids bringing up her name, but Kayla was a huge part of all our lives, and it feels unnatural not to bring her into the conversation."

I reached over and grabbed Carrie's hand. "It's okay to talk about her. I can't promise I won't get teary when someone does, but she was part of the Summer Six in the past, and she will continue to be part of the Summer Six into the future."

"Even if the Summer Six is now only four?" she asked about the six girls who had formed a club of sorts.

"Even if. We didn't stop talking about Peggy even after she…"

After she what? I asked myself. *After she ran away, after she was kidnapped, after she died?* The not knowing was the worst part.

"After she was no longer a part of our lives," Carrie supplied. "And yes, you are correct, we didn't stop talking about her. In fact, in the beginning, we talked about her more than we ever had before. It's just that…"

"It's just that you are being sensitive of my feelings," I provided. "And I appreciate that. But Kayla is gone, and that's something I need to learn to live with. Maybe if I talk about her enough, eventually, it won't hurt quite so much to do so." Even as I said that, I knew it wasn't true, but one could hope. "When are Nora and Quinn getting here?"

"Quinn is flying in from Paris and wasn't sure about all the connections, so she didn't have an ETA, though she said she'd be getting into San Francisco tomorrow, or possibly even the following day. I guess she'll make arrangements for the ferry over to the island once she arrives."

"So she probably won't be here until Monday at least."

"That would be my guess. You know how busy she is. I'm just grateful she agreed to take any time off at all."

Diana "Quinn" Quinby was a foreign correspondent for United Press International and traveled extensively. Although I hadn't seen her in years, I did chat with her on the phone every couple of months, and it seemed she lived an interesting life.

"And Nora?"

"Nora had to postpone her arrival and won't make it to the island until next week as well," Carrie continued. "I'm guessing Thursday or even Friday."

"I'm sorry to hear that. What happened?" Nora was married, with four grown children. She'd married her one true love, Matt Hargrove, right out of high school. Of all the couples I knew, they, it seemed, were the most perfectly suited.

"Shelby has been having some sort of issue with her college admissions packet, and Nora decided to make the trip out to Massachusetts to get it worked out in person. You know Nora; when it comes to those children of hers, a phone call won't do."

"I heard Shelby had been accepted to Harvard. That is really something. Nora must be over the moon with pride and happiness."

Carrie gently nibbled on her lower lip in what seemed to be a nervous habit. "You would think that Nora would be ecstatic that not only has Shelby actually achieved her dream of going to Harvard but, now that she will be going off to college, Matt and Nora would finally have the house to themselves. But when I spoke to her, she didn't seem happy. She seemed frantic and nervous and sort of sad."

"Sad?"

"I get the empty nest thing," Carrie shared. "I began to have all sorts of stress-related issues the moment Jessica started applying to colleges, and then, when she actually left the house where we'd raised her for the last time, I broke down and wept, despite the fact that I knew she'd be back for Christmas break. But I sensed something more than empty nest syndrome from Nora. Shelby is her youngest, and she has said goodbye to three other children. Still, I suppose the last one to leave home is the hardest."

"I guess we can talk to her to see what's on her mind when she gets here," I suggested.

"Yes, we can. I can't wait until we are all together again."

"I'm excited to see everyone, but sitting here relaxing with you is nice, too," I said. "I'd forgotten how blue the sea is along this stretch of beach."

"It is something special," she agreed. "I always did think this was the prettiest stretch of coastline on the island. I've even thought of buying one of the little cottages down the road after I sell my house."

"You're selling your house? That's great. When I spoke to you last, you sounded like you weren't ready to make the break."

She nodded. "I used to love that house, but part of my new life, new me plan includes a new living space. I still want to be on the water, but I want something small that I can maintain with minimal effort. I haven't definitely decided to move to this end of the island because there are advantages to being close to the village, but I have definitely decided to sell the house. Carl is having a fit about that, but to be perfectly honest, I don't care. I got the house in the divorce settlement, so it is mine to do with as I please."

I held up my glass in a toast. "Good for you. I love your new life, new you mantra. I think it is exactly the attitude you need to move past this and get on with whatever the future holds."

Carrie clicked her glass with mine. "I was a total wreck for a long time, but I really do feel better with each day that passes. I actually feel excited to see what comes next for me." Her phone buzzed. She looked at the caller ID. "It's a text from Jessica, letting me know that she made it to France."

"Jessica is in France?"

Carrie nodded. "I'd hoped she'd spend the summer here on the island, but she insisted that she'd made plans with a friend to tour Europe. I know it's been hard on her since Carl and I split up, so I didn't really blame her for not wanting to hang out in the war zone, but I sure do miss her. Now that Carl is no longer in my life, I feel sort of empty."

"I'm sure that will get better with time."

"I'm sure it will." She smiled. "In fact, it already has. Since it is just the two of us tonight, should we head into the village to see if we can break some hearts?"

I laughed. "I don't know about the breaking hearts part, but I'd love to have dinner in the village. Is Danello's still there?"

"It is, and they still have the best Italian food you are going to get anywhere."

"It's been forever since I allowed myself that many carbs, but I'm game if you are."

"Oh, I'm game." Carrie stood up. "Just let me change, and we'll go."

Books by Kathi Daley
Come for the murder, stay for the romance

The Inn at Holiday Bay:
Boxes in the Basement
Letters in the Library
Message in the Mantel
Answers in the Attic
Haunting in the Hallway
Pilgrim in the Parlor
Note in the Nutcracker
Blizzard in the Bay
Proof in the Photo
Gossip in the Garden – *June 2020*

A Cat in the Attic Mystery:
The Curse of Hollister House
The Mystery Before Christmas
The Case of the Cupid Caper
The Secret of Logan Pond

Reunion Trilogy — Island Reunion
Summerhouse Reunion
Topsail Sundays – *May 2020*
Campfire Secrets – *June 2020*

Zoe Donovan Cozy Mystery:
Halloween Hijinks
The Trouble With Turkeys
Christmas Crazy
Cupid's Curse

Big Bunny Bump-off
Beach Blanket Barbie
Maui Madness
Derby Divas
Haunted Hamlet
Turkeys, Tuxes, and Tabbies
Christmas Cozy
Alaskan Alliance
Matrimony Meltdown
Soul Surrender
Heavenly Honeymoon
Hopscotch Homicide
Ghostly Graveyard
Santa Sleuth
Shamrock Shenanigans
Kitten Kaboodle
Costume Catastrophe
Candy Cane Caper
Holiday Hangover
Easter Escapade
Camp Carter
Trick or Treason
Reindeer Roundup
Hippity Hoppity Homicide
Firework Fiasco
Henderson House
Holiday Hostage
Lunacy Lake
Celtic Christmas
Dija Diva – *Summer 2020*

Zimmerman Academy The New Normal
Zimmerman Academy New Beginnings
Ashton Falls Cozy Cookbook

Whales and Tails Cozy Mystery:

Romeow and Juliet
The Mad Catter
Grimm's Furry Tail
Much Ado About Felines
Legend of Tabby Hollow
Cat of Christmas Past
A Tale of Two Tabbies
The Great Catsby
Count Catula
The Cat of Christmas Present
A Winter's Tail
The Taming of the Tabby
Frankencat
The Cat of Christmas Future
Farewell to Felines
A Whisker in Time
The Catsgiving Feast
A Whale of a Tail
The Catnap Before Christmas
A Mew Beginning

A Tess and Tilly Mystery:

The Christmas Letter
The Valentine Mystery
The Mother's Day Mishap
The Halloween House
The Thanksgiving Trip
The Saint Paddy's Promise
The Halloween Haunting
The Christmas Clause
The Wedding Plan – *Summer 2020*

Rescue Alaska Mystery:

Finding Justice
Finding Answers
Finding Courage
Finding Christmas
Finding Shelter – *Fall 2020*

The Hathaway Sisters:

Harper
Harlow
Hayden – *Coming Soon*

Writers' Retreat Mystery:

First Case
Second Look
Third Strike
Fourth Victim
Fifth Night
Sixth Cabin
Seventh Chapter
Eighth Witness
Ninth Grave

Haunting by the Sea:

Homecoming by the Sea
Secrets by the Sea
Missing by the Sea
Betrayal by the Sea
Thanksgiving by the Sea
Christmas by the Sea

Tj Jensen Paradise Lake Mystery:

Pumpkins in Paradise
Snowmen in Paradise
Bikinis in Paradise
Christmas in Paradise
Puppies in Paradise
Halloween in Paradise
Treasure in Paradise
Fireworks in Paradise
Beaches in Paradise
Thanksgiving in Paradise

Sand and Sea Hawaiian Mystery:

Murder at Dolphin Bay
Murder at Sunrise Beach
Murder at the Witching Hour
Murder at Christmas
Murder at Turtle Cove
Murder at Water's Edge
Murder at Midnight
Murder at Pope Investigations

Seacliff High Mystery:

The Secret
The Curse
The Relic
The Conspiracy
The Grudge
The Shadow
The Haunting

Road to Christmas Romance:

Road to Christmas Past

USA Today best-selling author Kathi Daley lives in beautiful Lake Tahoe with her husband Ken. When she isn't writing, she likes spending time hiking the miles of desolate trails surrounding her home. She has authored more than a hundred books in twelve series. Find out more about her books at www.kathidaley.com

Stay up-to-date:
Newsletter, *The Daley Weekly* http://eepurl.com/NRPDf
Webpage – www.kathidaley.com
Facebook at Kathi Daley Books –
www.facebook.com/kathidaleybooks
Kathi Daley Books Group Page –
https://www.facebook.com/groups/569578823146850/
E-mail – kathidaley@kathidaley.com
Twitter at Kathi Daley@kathidaley –
https://twitter.com/kathidaley
Amazon Author Page –
https://www.amazon.com/author/kathidaley
BookBub – https://www.bookbub.com/authors/kathi-daley

Made in the USA
Middletown, DE
20 September 2020

20247676R00120